THE BRUMBACK LIBRARY
OF VAN WERT COUNTY
VAN WERT OHIO

Desert Magic

DESERT MAGIC

ALICE SHARPE

AVALON BOOKS
THOMAS BOUREGY AND COMPANY, INC.
401 LAFAYETTE STREET
NEW YORK, NEW YORK 10003

ROM
F
SHA

GR RP

PRINTED IN THE UNITED STATES OF AMERICA
ON ACID-FREE PAPER
BY HADDON CRAFTSMEN, SCRANTON, PENNSYLVANIA

To C. Dell Turney

Chapter One

D avis Todd couldn't believe it. He rolled down the truck window and would have rubbed his eyes to make sure the desert sun hadn't conjured up a mirage if right at that second the object of his scrutiny hadn't turned to face him before she ducked inside Wheeler's Handi-Mart.

He ducked into the shadow provided by the visor and let his breath escape in a long, low whistle, even though the woman he gazed at with a growing sense of inevitability couldn't possibly have seen him from clear across the street. He realized he might never have recognized her if it weren't for the defiant tilt of her chin, which brought back so many memories, and the radiant wave of copper hair that still cascaded down her back.

''Nancy . . .'' he mumbled to himself, his voice a

mixture of wonder and longing even he wasn't aware of. "What are you doing back in Sage?"

"This is all you want?" the woman behind the counter asked. She was a tall, thin redhead, hovering near fifty and almost looking it.

"That's all," Nan said.

"People buy the funniest things. Take your purchase. Three cans of soup and a jar of dill pickles? What kind of meal can you build on that?"

"Lunch for my father," Nan explained, smiling to herself as she always did when confronted with the inconsistency of a chef—of sorts—preferring canned soup to the homemade variety.

The woman rang up the purchases. Nan heard herself asking, "Does JoJo Wheeler still own the store?"

"Ms. Wheeler sold out two, maybe three years ago. Did you know her?"

"I used to live here," Nan said softly. She'd been away from Sage for a few days short of five years. Walking into the store, she'd been struck with how little things had changed, but she realized now that that impression was deceptive. JoJo was gone, and she'd been a fixture of Nan's childhood, dispensing penny licorice and jawbreakers along with advice for a skinny, motherless child.

For old times' sake Nan selected a piece of licorice. "This too," she added, taking a bite. She hadn't had licorice since she left Sage the summer after high-school graduation. The licorice tasted like dusty streets, allowance day, and long summer nights, all rolled into one.

"That'll be $6.92," the clerk said.

Nan didn't wince over the cost, but as she looked through her wallet for the money, she did decide that in the future she was going to have to master the stick shift of her father's aged panel truck and drive into Reno for supplies.

"I'll have to write a check," Nan said. She handed it to the clerk, who studied the Oregon address with suspicion. Nan said, "My father lives in town. He owns the diner down the street, the Cactus Cup."

The clerk's eyes crackled with sudden curiosity. "You're the Hillman girl? Good grief, you came back!"

"I beg your pardon—"

"My goodness! I'm Marjorie Block," she added, sticking out her right hand. "Never figured I'd meet you!"

As Nan shook the woman's hand, she scrutinized the vivid face, struck by remarks that hinted at knowledge the woman couldn't possibly possess. She finally said, "I'm sorry, but I don't understand."

"Time to let bygones be bygones. The past belongs to yesterday, that's what I always say. Besides, now with your daddy's leg in a cast—"

Nan lost the thread of what Marjorie Block was saying because she was too busy trying to figure out where the information had come from. When Marjorie paused to catch her breath, Nan said, "You know my father well?"

"Oh, honey, you have been away, haven't you? Blink twice while you're driving through, and you miss Sage—remember? I wouldn't say I know your daddy well, but fact of the matter is I know everyone in town at least to nod to, and I've only been here two years. I used to deal blackjack in Reno, but that's another story entirely. Besides, I have breakfast in your father's diner every Tuesday. It won't be the same, what with Harry Mule behind the counter instead of your dad. Know what I mean?"

"Yes," Nan said. She studied her hands and added, "Are you friends with Kyle Todd too?" As far as Nan knew, Kyle Todd was the only person in town who knew the details of what had driven Nan out of town so long before. The man had promised he wouldn't prosecute Nan if she left; he'd actually gone further than that. He'd promised he'd never tell another living soul what had happened if she left quietly, quickly, and permanently. Nan had left—quietly, quickly, and, she had thought, permanently.

To her consternation, Marjorie Block shrugged coyly. "As a matter of fact, Kyle and I are friends, if you know what I mean. Now, don't you worry, honey. I won't blab your secret."

Nan felt raging flames consume her cheeks while her stomach twisted like a wet dish towel. She grabbed her bag and hastily retreated to the relative privacy of the sidewalk, where she spent a few seconds breathing deeply, her back against the building, her eyes closed while she fought to regain a measure of control.

Kyle Todd had told Marjorie Block what had happened! At first the knowledge made Nan want to run again, but gradually the fear was replaced with fury. How dare he! For ten cents she'd march into his pharmacy and—

She made herself stand still, made herself concentrate on the sidewalk. Eventually the June heat seeping out of Main Street tempered her anger. She looked around to see if anyone had witnessed her temporary loss of control and found the sidewalk mostly empty. The few hardy souls who did wander out in the late-morning heat paid Nan no attention.

Sage was a small town aptly named for its major flora, which crowded next to every building, the gray-green shapes deceptively round and fuzzy looking. Larger, darker scrub brush added variety, and an occasional cottonwood tree announced a moist spot, but mostly it was sage and reddish-brown dirt, heavy on the sandy side.

The town itself had boomed twenty years before and now existed mainly as a place between Reno and nowhere, its new claim to fame a tool factory a few miles from the Truckee River. The factory hadn't been there when Nan left Sage.

She walked along the sidewalk, turning her face

away as she passed strangers, relieved when no one looked twice at her. Since she had walked into town fifteen minutes earlier, her fantasy of the past being buried under a thick blanket of time had evaporated like a drop of cold water on her father's cooking griddle. There was absolutely no way around it: Kyle Todd had told. He'd broken his promise.

In Nan's wildest dreams she'd never thought she'd come back to Sage, and even walking its streets, passing familiar storefronts, she wished she could change into a bird and fly away, back to the Oregon coast and what was now for her the real world, back to cool summers, her own apartment, her own life.

She looked up in time to see she was close to Todd's Pharmacy. She toyed with the idea of marching into Kyle's store and announcing her presence, demanding to know why he'd told Marjorie Block about the . . . incident. That was how she thought of that confrontation in the pharmacy—as an incident, an awful incident she'd been too young and too naive to really comprehend.

For a second Nan was eighteen years old again, standing in front of Kyle Todd, her boss, as he produced a man Nan now realized must have been in the throes of drug withdrawal. At the time she'd attributed his shaking hands and rapid blinking to nervousness.

She still remembered the shock of his knowing her name. He wasn't much older than she, just four or five years, but his jaw needed shaving, and his clothes hung on his tall frame as they would on an old man. He'd looked into her eyes and said, ''She's the one. Nancy Hillman, that's her. She sold 'em to me Friday night. She was alone here. 'Course, it wasn't the first time—''

Without realizing she'd done it, Nan had left the sidewalk and made her way to the street, attempting to escape the image she'd fought to forget.

She shouldn't have come back. . . .

Nothing short of her dad's accident would have brought her home, she reminded herself. It had been over eighteen months since his last visit to Oregon, a trip he'd made with frequency the first three and a half years of her exile, and when his call for help came, how could she refuse? He'd broken his leg in an automobile accident on County Road 36 two days before; that he hadn't killed himself was more a matter of luck than anything else. Nan had seen pictures of the late-model Chevy taken for the insurance company, and she had no idea how her father had climbed out of the crumbled front seat alive.

The question in Nan's mind was how her dad had ended up in a ditch on a perfectly straight piece of road in the first place. Had he been drinking? He swore he hadn't, and Sheriff Berry hadn't cited him for driving under the influence. Could he have suffered a stroke? She'd asked Boris, his lifelong friend and retired doctor, that question the night before. ''No indication of one," he'd assured her. "Accidents do happen, Nan."

So, Clive Hillman needed help. Nan had two brothers, but Steve had recently transplanted his family to California, and Rocky, her older brother, could barely keep food on his own table, let alone set up a housekeeping schedule for their father. It was up to Nan to leave her sixth-grade class for a week or so and make her way south. She'd thought it would be safe now, that Kyle Todd would never even know she'd come back to town and that maybe even if he did find out, he would have put the whole thing behind him just as she'd tried to do. Now to discover he'd told Marjorie Block their secret! How long would it be before Marjorie told Kyle that Nan was back in town, and what would happen when she did?

And what about Davis? At the thought of him, Nan's stomach twisted again. At least he'd be living far away from Sage by now and she wouldn't have to face him.

A horn honking broke her thoughts, and she looked up to see a dusty white car coming down the street. She stepped out of the way, but the car swerved close and came to a stop beside her. She looked down at the driver.

"Paul? Paul Avery?"

"Nan Hillman, as I live and breathe! I swear, I can't believe it's you. Last time we talked, you were on your way out of town and you were never coming back!''

Nan's smile wilted. ''Well, Dad hurt his leg—''

''I heard about that. Are you heading out to his place now? Do you need a lift?''

She nodded. ''I'd love a ride.'' She came around and got into the car. She put the small sack of groceries between her feet and turned to face Paul.

Wow! she thought. *He's changed*. When they'd graduated from high school, he'd been a gawky kid with a thatch of red hair. The hair had darkened and curled; his tall frame had filled in. *He looks good.*

''You're still as pretty as ever,'' Paul said. He cast her a quick sidelong look and added, ''I bet you still won't go out on a date with me even if I ask you real nice.''

She laughed. ''I thought you were married to Alison Parker.''

''Alison died late last year,'' he said curtly.

Shocked, Nan mumbled, ''I'm sorry, Paul. I didn't know.''

He shook his head and spared her a quick, apologetic smile. ''I forgot Steve moved away and that your dad and Rocky probably don't write much. It's me who's sorry. I shouldn't have bitten your head off.''

''It's okay,'' she assured him. She glanced at him, wondering if he would mind explaining what had happened to Alison, but the knot in his jaw made her hold her tongue. Maybe he was thinking of Alison. Quiet, pretty Alison, one of Nan's best friends, lost to Nan because of an addict's accusations.

Or was that fair? She hadn't had the nerve to stay and fight when she knew she was innocent. She hadn't had the guts to face what Davis would think of her if his father told him what he claimed to have proof to support, proof beyond the addict's word. She'd decided to flee instead of fight, and if she'd lost everything in the bargain, wasn't that her own fault?

She kept silent as Paul drove the two miles out to Clive Hillman's place. They passed Steve's old mobile home, rented now by a woman with four children, all boys, two of whom seemed to be waging battle over possession of a rusty bike, and then they drove past an oddly shaped parcel of sandy earth with nothing on it except the inevitable sagebrush and a large, rectangular black spot.

Paul said, "Have you seen Davis Todd since you've been back?"

"He's here?" she asked, alarmed.

"Sure."

"But I thought—"

"That he went away and became a hotshot doctor? Nope. He flunked out and came back to town with his tail between his legs. So, I guess you haven't seen him yet."

Nan felt as though all of the air were being sucked

out of her lungs. If only her infatuation with Davis hadn't been such common knowledge in Sage! She could still remember the first time she heard the rumor they were getting married. She and Davis had been in Tucker's hardware store buying some kind of woodworking tool when the clerk had said, "I hear you two are getting married next week. Congratulations!"

Nan had wanted to die. She'd looked up at Davis to see how he was taking this piece of misinformation, ready to tell the clerk that it was nonsense, that while Davis had graduated from college, he still had years of medical school ahead of him and she was going to junior college in Reno. Davis's grin silenced her.

He'd tightened his grip on her hand and said, "Can't always believe everything you hear."

"You mean you're not getting married?" the clerk asked.

Davis shrugged. "Now, if you can't believe what you hear, what's the use of my telling you whether we are or not? Better wait until it comes out in the newspaper."

"Can't believe everything you read, either," Nan said and was rewarded with another grin from Davis.

The clerk handed over the gadget. "You two belong together."

Later, outside the store, Davis swung her into his

arms and said, "He's right, you know. We do belong together."

"After you become a doctor," Nan had said.

He'd answered her by staring at their linked hands and then smiling. "Yeah," he'd said. "After I become a doctor."

"Nan?" Paul asked. "You okay?"

She had been so completely lost in the past that for a moment she wasn't even sure where she was. She stared at Paul a second, forced a weary smile onto her face, and said, "I rode the bus all night, and I guess I'm more tired than I thought."

"You and Davis were a hot item back when."

"I've only been here for a little over twenty-four hours," she replied breezily. "You're about the first person outside Dad and Boris that I've really spoken to."

"Boris Griswold? Is he still practicing medicine?"

"Not officially, but as soon as Dad hurt himself, he called Boris. I guess the doctor in Reno does all the work and Boris takes all the credit."

Paul nodded. "About Davis—"

"As far as I'm concerned, Davis Todd belongs to the past."

Paul shifted into a lower gear and crawled down the ledge toward the river, a smile on his lips. He pulled the car up beside the one-story house Nan had grown up in and said, "Can't come in to say hello to Clive because I have a meeting in Reno in an hour. Tell him I miss him at the Cactus Cup.''

''Okay.''

''And, Nan,'' he added, catching her arm, ''I really am sorry I snapped at you earlier. Actually, I'm real glad you're back in Sage. I always wondered why you left so quickly and never came back. Heck, you didn't even write anyone here, did you? I know Alison never got a letter.''

''I . . . I was real . . . busy,'' she mumbled.

He nodded. ''What are the chances you'd consider coming to dinner with me tomorrow night? We have a lot of catching up to do.''

''I'd say the chances are pretty good.''

''Really? Great. I'll give you a call.''

''Thanks for the ride,'' she called as he gunned his engine to make it back up the hill.

Her dad's house had once been bright yellow, but sunlight and time had conspired to fade the paint. An old wooden wagon wheel leaned against the front porch railing; weeds grew up and under the porch floor, beaten down in front of the door by human feet. The screens were torn, the shutters either missing or crooked, the whole building covered with a hazy layer of gritty dirt. A few cottonwood trees shaded the house and ran down toward the river, their leaves rustling in the late-morning breeze.

Nan thought the trees were the only vivid-looking thing around and wondered if she'd have the time and energy to throw a new coat of paint on the house before she arranged for permanent help for her father and escaped Sage again.

The screen door slammed behind her. In the instant before it did, she took a mental picture of her father sitting at the table. Clive Hillman was two months shy of sixty-eight, a full-bodied man with a comfortable face deeply etched with what he referred to as "character lines." His hair was a salt-and-pepper shag, heavy on the salt, his skin well tanned despite the hours he spent behind the counter at the Cactus Cup, his big hands a little bent now with arthritis. He sat hunched over a cordless phone, his gaze directed inward, his left leg in a cast, the cast propped on another chair, his crutches on the floor.

The door slammed, his head swiveled around to face her, and Nan realized that the pose she'd interpreted as peaceful introspection was actually seething anger.

"That . . . that . . . that blasted Harry Mule!"

"Now, Dad—"

"Do you know what that imbecile has gone and done now?"

"I know you need some lunch," Nan said, attempting to placate him. "What kind of soup do you want—tomato, clam chowder, barley beef?"

"He went and blew himself up!"

She stopped unpacking groceries. "What?"

"Said the second burner on the gas grill didn't start

up, so he decided to lean down and take a peek. Got his face right next to the pilot and boom! The thing blew.''

''Is he all right?''

''I guess he lost his eyebrows and the front of that fancy toupee he went and bought. Can you believe it?''

''But, Dad, is Harry hurt?''

''Oh, he's okay, which goes to prove God watches over idiots.''

Nan studied her father's face closely, relieved when his frown began to tremble until it dissolved into a smirk that was quickly followed by a series of protracted hoots and a chuckle that brought tears to his eyes. ''Picture old Harry with no eyebrows,'' he said at last.

''Poor man,'' she said as she stirred the tomato soup she'd dumped into a saucepan, but she was smiling too.

''Poor man, my foot,'' Clive said, wiping tears from his eyes with his fingers. ''He's worked at the Cactus Cup off and on for six years, Nan, and I swear, he's as big a klutz now as he was the first time I left him there alone. Remember that? It was the time I drove up to see you, right after you moved in with your Aunt Carolyn. Harry threw out all my silverware when he scraped the plates. He said it was a mistake, but I know it was because he hated washing the darned things.''

"Then why did you ask him to cover for you, Dad? Isn't there someone else?"

"Are you kidding? Except for me, he's the only one dumb enough to work his tail off for nothing. I just hope he leaves the diner in one piece. I tell you, Nan, I've got to get back on my feet soon."

"Settle down, Dad." She ladled soup into a bowl, garnishing the accompanying plate with a dill-pickle slice and a fan of crackers. "How's it feel to have someone serve you lunch for a change?" she asked as she set it in front of him.

"Just fine, honey. You know how much I appreciate your coming back here to help me out for a few days. 'Course, I never did really understand why you wouldn't come back even for a visit, why it was always me that had to go to Oregon to see you. Now, honey, don't get that trapped look on your pretty face. I know you must have had your reasons. Well, now, how was town? See anyone you used to know?"

She sat down opposite him and took a steadying breath. "Paul Avery gave me a ride home. I didn't know his wife died. You never told me."

"Didn't I? Well, it was a terrible thing about Alison, just terrible. She and Paul bought the place between Steve's land and mine a few years ago. They put one of those double-wide mobile homes on it like your brother did. Fire marshal decided Alison fell asleep with a cigarette in her fingers, and the rest is history.''

Nan thought of the horrible black spot on the land next to Steve's. Paul had driven right past it. She shuddered and said, ''How awful!''

Clive took a sip of soup. ''She was a nice girl. She and Steve's wife got pretty close. It was hard on Donna when Alison died.''

''And Paul.''

Her father grunted. ''Did you see anyone else?''

''I didn't know JoJo Wheeler had sold out and left town. You want me to heat that soup for you, Dad?''

''No, thanks, honey. I don't seem to have much of an appetite today. Aren't you having any?''

''I never did develop a fondness for canned soup,'' she confessed. The mention of JoJo reminded Nan of the knowing comments made by Marjorie Block. She swallowed a hard lump that materialized in her throat. Kyle had promised not to tell anyone, but obviously he'd broken the promise. The question now was, how many times had he broken it? Was there a possibility her father knew? Did Davis?

''JoJo didn't leave town,'' Clive said suddenly. ''She bought a place out beyond that new tool factory and got herself a few dogs, a couple of cats, and a horse. She'd love to see you, Nan. I should have invited her over to dinner tonight. Did I tell you Rocky and Boris are coming? I think there's chicken in the freezer.''

''I already put two in the fridge to defrost.''

She resolutely put her fears behind her. She wasn't eighteen any longer. She was a full-grown woman of twenty-three, with one year of teaching thirty kids behind her and a whole future ahead. The past was the past. Besides, if her father knew about what happened, he'd say something. Clive Hillman wasn't the kind of man to tolerate an injustice to his only daughter without leaping to the rescue.

For the millionth time Nan wished she'd confided ''the incident'' to her father, had allowed him to help her. At the time, she reminded herself, it had seemed hopeless, and perhaps, to the eighteen-year-old Nan, there had seemed more to lose by fighting than by running.

As for Davis? Well, she'd long ago given up any hope of making things right between him and her. If Kyle had told him what he accused Nan of doing, then at least now Davis knew why she'd left. It didn't matter; it was out of her control.

''Well, how about it?'' Clive asked for the third time. ''You see anyone you know? I mean besides Paul.''

Narrowing her eyes, Nan said, ''No one else. What are you getting at, Dad?''

His spoon rattled against the bowl as he glanced quickly at Nan. ''Me? Nothing. Just asking.''

Before she could investigate further, a knock sounded at the door, and she twirled around in her seat to face it. In this way she laid her eyes on Davis Todd for the first time in four years, three hundred and twenty-one days.

She was not prepared for the way her heart slowly began beating again after just as long a time.

Chapter Two

"Nancy," Davis said quietly.

Nan jumped to her feet. She stared at him through the screen door, aware of little more than the intensity of his gaze and the slow thudding of her heart in her chest. Gradually details flooded her brain—straight dark hair combed back from a high forehead, winter-blue eyes, lean features, square jaw.

Davis. He'd be every day of twenty-nine years old now, she thought, wearing his years the way some men do, right there on the surface for the world to see, yet somehow better for the passing time.

Nan felt as though reality had skipped out the door, leaving her alone in a dream—a familiar dream where she confronted the first man she'd ever loved. How many times had she rehearsed what she'd say, what he'd say, how he'd look? But that had been years ago. The dreams had stopped, and she'd figured she was over Davis Todd. Only, now that she was here, and now that he was standing on the other side of the screen door, she found it wasn't that simple.

"Davis," she said at last, "what are you doing here?"

"What do you think?"

Taking a deep breath, she said, "I think you should have let things be."

She heard a noise behind her shoulder. Clive had struggled to his feet and managed to grab his crutches. "That's no way to treat a guest, Nan. I asked Davis over. Come on in, boy."

Nan looked down at the floor. She wished Davis would come inside, and she wished he would go away. She honestly didn't know which wish was the stronger. What she did know was that she couldn't bear to be in the same room with him.

Staring at Nan, he said, "How about it, Nancy? May I come inside?"

She shrugged. She'd always loved the way he refused to shorten her name, the soft inflection in his voice on that hard first consonant.

Davis opened the door and stepped inside. Without the filter of the screen, he came into sharper focus. The desert sun had etched fine lines around his eyes and cut new angles on his cheekbones. His hair was long in the back, caught in the collar of a blue chambray shirt rolled up at the sleeves, an unbuttoned suede vest emphasizing the wide breadth of his shoulders. He was wearing dusty jeans and worn leather boots. His fingers were long, sensitive looking—a doctor's hands, Kyle Todd had often bragged. *Good grief,* she thought in a wave of pity for Davis. How Kyle must have exploded when his son failed medical school!

"It's good to see you," Davis said.

Nan nodded. "It's . . . good . . . to see you too," she answered and then left her father and Davis to discuss whatever it was they were meeting to discuss. The screen door slammed behind her.

She kicked rocks all the way down to the river, where she leaned against a cottonwood tree, so different from the pines and redwoods in Oregon, and stared at the tumbling water. Upstream, a muskrat paddled against the current, and several sea gulls, a long way from the sea, landed on a scattering of rocks.

She closed her eyes against the beauty and tried to clear her mind.

Five years, and yet the sight of him could make her breath catch, could make her palms sweat, could rekindle an ache in her heart she'd thought was long extinguished. Why was he here? She opened her eyes and glanced back at the house. An old truck with a fiberglass shell on the back was parked in back of her dad's van; obviously Davis was still inside. She pushed herself away from the tree and approached the water.

The river was wide at this point, at least twenty feet, maybe more. It tumbled and rushed over basketball-sized rocks, pooling near the shore. Nan made her way over the rocks until she found one flat enough to kneel on. She knelt down, hooked her long hair behind her ears, and scooped handfuls of cold water to splash onto her face. The water trickled down her neck, leaving large, dark splotches on her yellow shirt. She didn't care; she just wanted to wash Davis Todd out of her head.

"Nancy?"

Thanks to the noise the river made as it rushed past her, she hadn't heard him approach. In one not-so-fluid movement, she stood, twirled around, lost her balance, and began falling. Big hands caught her elbows, effortlessly righted her. She didn't dare look up, but the sight of his hands on her arms sent pangs of longing through her chest.

"You're standing in the river," he said from his perch atop the rock.

She looked down at her feet; sure enough, six inches of river water flowed over her shoes. Davis dropped his hands, and they both retreated to the shore.

Nan pushed her hair away from her face and sighed. She hardly recognized her voice when she said, "Davis, I don't know what to say to you. You shouldn't have come."

"Don't you want to talk about the weather or tell

me how pretty Oregon is this time of year?'' he asked.
''Don't look so surprised. I know you went to Oregon.
I know you're a teacher now. Fact is, I know a lot
about you, Nancy Hillman. Darn near the only thing
I don't know is why you ran out on me five years
ago.''

Nan shook her head and took a few steps away
from him, her wet shoes squeaking as she moved
across the rocks. She turned around again and found
he'd followed. She was shocked by the intensity of
the desire she felt to tell him what had happened.
Only the growing fear of what was ahead for her kept
her from blurting out the truth, that she'd adored him
and would never have left him if she hadn't been
forced to.

But if Kyle had told Marjorie Block about ''the
incident,'' it proved it was still alive in his mind.
What would happen when he discovered she'd come
back to Sage? What would happen if he chose to
prosecute her? Even if she were found innocent, what
would the school board back at home think of a
teacher accused of selling amphetamines to an addict?

And what would all this do to Davis? Would he
believe his father, that Nan had used him to get the
job at the pharmacy, that she'd never cared for him,
that the whole thing had been an act? She put her fist
against her temple in a feeble attempt to still the
beginning throbs of a headache.

"There's nothing I can tell you that you don't already know," she said at last.

He nodded, his face stern. "I see."

"Wouldn't it be better if we just put this in the past? I mean, there's really nothing left to say."

"That's not true," he said slowly. "I figure we have a whole lot to say to each other."

Nan took a deep breath. "We were kids."

"I thought we were in love."

"Puppy love," Nan said. "Those things run down eventually. You know how it is."

He shook his head. "I don't believe a word of this, Nancy. You know darn good and well that what we had was more than puppy love. Do you have any idea how worried I was when you vanished off the face of the earth like that? I looked everywhere for you. If Rocky hadn't finally told me you'd gone off to live with your Aunt Carolyn in Oregon, I'd have gone mad. I did what you told Rocky you wanted me to do—I left you alone. But now you're back, and now I want to know why you left the way you did."

Nan shook her head; at least Kyle hadn't told Davis what he'd told Marjorie Block. "I'm sorry," she said, her voice shaking—with tension or relief, she wasn't sure which. "There really isn't anything more to say about it."

He extended his hand toward her shoulder, but after a quick glance at her face withdrew it. "You don't understand," he said at last. "You don't understand the way I felt—"

"I do understand," she interrupted, turning away again. She felt his hand on her shoulder and tried not to tremble.

"That's hard for me to believe." His voice was a soft caress.

"It all happened so long ago," Nan said for what felt like the twentieth time.

Davis turned her to face him. He looked into her eyes and said, "I was hurt. I was in love with you. My father said you didn't want to see me. I didn't believe him, but then when Rocky said the same thing, it began to sink in that you really didn't want anything to do with me. It was all so sudden."

Nan looked away. Finally she said, "I know I could have been nicer about the way I left, but believe me when I tell you that I never intended to hurt you."

He frowned slightly, his forehead wrinkling as he thought. It was a gesture of concentration that Nan remembered well. At last he said, "You didn't mean to hurt me?"

"No." She took a deep breath and added, "Besides, we're different people now. What does the past matter?"

"The past always matters," he said, his voice introspective.

"But it seems so far away, as if it was another lifetime."

"Does it really seem that far away to you?" Davis asked, narrowing his eyes.

Nan returned his gaze. She swallowed and lied through her teeth. "Yes, of course it does," she said.

"Then we can relegate the whole thing to the past?"

Nan wasn't sure she could. If Kyle was telling people she'd broken the law, the matter was hardly in the past. In fact, the longer she stayed in Sage, the better the chance something would come of it. However, she'd agree to almost anything if it would get Davis to take his hands off her shoulders, to stop looking inside of her.

"Okay," she said.

He nodded. "Where would you like to go for dinner?"

"Oh, no. No, Davis."

His hands dropped to his sides. "So it's not in the past. The whole thing is right here between us. You left without a word, and now you're back, and you still won't talk. Even if we can't go back to where we were—"

"We most certainly cannot go back to where we were—" Nan interrupted, but he held up his hand and continued.

"Like I said, even if we can't go back to where we were, it would be nice if we could be friendly to each other."

"Why?"

He looked skyward, then back down into her eyes. "Because of your father. He and I are pretty close."

Oh, great, Nan thought. *Oh, wonderful!*

Davis sighed heavily. "Listen, Nan, I didn't come here to argue with you. I just wanted to talk, to try to understand what happened. Come out with me. If not tonight, then tomorrow night."

"I'm busy tomorrow night," she said, suddenly very pleased that Paul had asked her to dinner. The temptation to drop her guard with Davis, to look at him the way her heart yearned to, to hold his hand to her cheek, melt into his arms, was too compelling. For her sake, and his, she had to resist.

"The night after then—"

"I'm busy," she repeated quickly.

He studied her face for a second. Nan made herself return his stare.

"Okay," he said at last. "But think about what I said. Maybe your schedule will miraculously open up. All I really want is the truth and not a bunch of evasions. All I'm asking for is a chance to talk to you."

"That's what we've been doing."

"No," he answered slowly. "We haven't really said a word to each other." Turning on his boot heels, he walked back toward the house and his truck while Nan watched his retreating figure. It wasn't until she saw him drive up the ravine that she took an unsteady breath.

* * *

"What was Davis doing here, Dad?" Nan asked as she washed a couple of aspirin down with a glass of water. She'd returned to the house to find her father glued to the screen door. He hobbled back to his chair and sat down wearily.

"You look like you're ready to cry, honey. You two fight? And how did your feet get all wet? You're dripping on the floor."

"Forget the floor. Why was he here?"

Clive chewed on the inside of his lower lip for a minute. Then he said, "Let me tell you something, Nan. Davis came into the Cactus Cup a couple of months ago. Now, as you know, I never did care much for the boy, or maybe I just assumed he'd be like his old man—I don't know. Anyway, when you two were dating each other, I thought Davis was too old and you were too young. There were only five years between you, but they were an important five years, especially for you."

"You were right."

"Maybe, maybe not. Anyway, I hadn't seen much of Davis since you left, and then one day he started coming into the diner, and we got to talking. He said my counter was sure a mess, and I had to agree with him. I hired him to rebuild part of it—he's a darn good finish carpenter. Well, actually, he's more than that. Anyway, we talked even more."

"Not about me!"

"No, young lady. Fascinating as you are, there are other things to talk about, though your name did come up now and again. I got to liking him, Nan. Besides, you know how I admire a skilled workman, and the boy is good."

Nan shook her head and said, "Can you imagine how furious Kyle Todd must be that his one and only son turned into a carpenter instead of a doctor? It must eat him up inside."

"You should see Davis's workshop, Nan. Don't belittle his occupation until you see what he's capable of."

"I wasn't belittling him, Dad," she explained. "I was just thinking of the way Kyle used to act, as though Davis completing medical school were the most important thing in the entire world. When Davis flunked out—"

"Wait a minute. Where did you hear that Davis flunked out?"

"Paul Avery said—"

"Does he know that for certain?"

"Well, I don't have any idea if he does or not, of course. I just assumed it was common knowledge."

"It's not," Clive said firmly. "Truth of the matter is that neither Davis nor Kyle will talk about what happened."

Nan nodded. She looked into her father's eyes and was startled to see the depth of fatigue that clouded his pupils. She smiled brightly, determined to change the subject to something pleasant. "How shall I cook the chicken tonight, Dad? That is, if you're still up to having guests."

"Your brother and Boris are hardly guests," he said. He sighed deeply and added, "You decide, Nan. Maybe I'll go take a short nap. . . ."

"Sure," she said and helped him retrieve his crutches from where he'd dropped them on the floor beneath the table. She helped him settle down on the couch with an afghan pulled up to his chin even though the outside temperature had to be in the nineties.

As she washed the chicken, she found herself wondering how she was going to handle seeing Davis again; maybe she'd be lucky and he wouldn't come around. Or maybe it would be easier the next time they met; maybe the intensity of their emotions would fade on repetition. That was something to hope for.

"You could be a world-class chef!" Boris said several hours later. Dinner was almost finished. They'd eaten in the kitchen, in front of two fans set up to circulate the air. Still, it was pretty warm and stuffy, and Nan sat back in her chair, fanning herself with her open hand.

She looked at Boris affectionately. He was as old as her father; in fact, they claimed they'd been ardent rivals for Nan's mother back in high school. Boris was inches shorter and inches wider than Clive, and his hair was jet black—thanks, Nan suspected, to Grecian Formula. His face was as round as a full moon, and his hair as sparse as cactus flowers in August. Two very shiny black eyes glowed in his face, and when he smiled, which he did often, he reminded Nan of a bald teddy bear.

"You're just saying that," Nan said.

"Nah, he's right," Rocky said around a mouthful of chicken paprika. "You cook pretty good, little sister."

Rocky was a young carbon copy of Clive—tall, slender, blond, lanky. The only thing he hadn't inherited from his father was the older man's drive and determination. Rocky was content to work on old cars, taking a small job here and there when the need arose.

"Thanks, Rocky," she said. He was like a stranger in some ways, Nan thought. A familiar stranger with a whole world going on behind his eyes, a world she wasn't privy to. She often felt that way with the children she taught, as though the major essence of their personality was locked inside their head and heart and part of the challenge was discovering it.

Clive coughed into his handkerchief, which won him a hurried glance from Boris. Nan noticed this and said, "What's wrong, Dad?"

Clive shook his head. "Honestly, it's getting so a man can't sputter once in a while without everyone throwing a fit!"

Nan looked at her father's plate. She'd served him herself, and though the food was scattered here and there, it didn't appear he'd eaten much. She said, "Are you sure you're okay?"

" 'Course I'm not okay! I got a broken leg, and maybe I'm getting a cold. I also got Harry Mule trying to blow up my diner and a daughter watching every darned thing I do. Did you tell Rocky and Boris about what Harry did today?"

As Nan repeated the story of the gas stove and Harry's missing eyebrows, she saw her dad swallow a couple of pills with what was left of his iced tea. She looked at Boris to see if he'd seen it, too, but he was staring at Rocky, who was busy shredding his napkin.

Nan finished the story and leaned toward her father. "Is something wrong with dinner?" she asked. "You've hardly eaten any—"

"Too much paprika," he said quickly.

"I used your recipe—"

"You'll learn, young lady, as you grow older, that a recipe is a progressive work of art."

"And your recipe for chicken paprika progressed past the need for paprika?"

"Yes," he said simply. "And the chicken is too dry," he added just as Rocky served himself a third helping.

Eventually Boris helped Clive maneuver himself into the living room for the ritualistic game of checkers. Nan leaned against the sink, weary beyond explanation until she realized she'd been in Sage only twelve hours and hadn't slept the night before on the bus, which pretty much explained why she now felt like sleeping for a week.

Rocky pushed a chair over to the counter and said, "I'll wash. You sit there and dry."

"Thanks."

"No problem," he said, holding his hand out in front of him. "I need to get this auto grease out from under my fingernails, anyway."

"How delightful!"

He grinned at Nan. "Only kidding."

Nan hadn't seen Rocky for almost five years because he was apparently as reluctant to leave Sage as she was to come home, and she was suddenly grief-stricken that this was yet another person she'd let slip out of her life. It hadn't seemed important when she was eighteen and Rocky was twenty-seven that she remain close to him. The nine years separating their ages meant they'd spent virtually their entire lives as strangers, anyway.

Now she watched him wash the dishes—in a manner of speaking—and felt remorse that their paths were soon to split yet again. Who knew how long it would be before she'd screw up her courage and come back to Sage for another visit? For that matter, who knew what was going to come of this visit?

At least she hadn't lost contact with her other

brother. Steve and his family came to Oregon every summer, like clockwork. "I'm not going to have my kids growing up without meeting their Aunt Nan," he'd said the last time she thanked him for coming. And now that he was in California, she could visit him. What would he think when she suddenly found the time and energy to visit California when she could find neither for returning to Nevada?

"You're quiet tonight, little sister," Rocky said as he handed her the chicken platter. It still had smudges of sauce on it. Nan didn't say anything, but she realized she was going to have to rewash all the dishes after he left.

She yawned and said, "I'm pooped."

"You see Davis Todd today?"

That name again. It was always there, on the tip of everyone's tongue, ready to spring off at any second and catch her unaware. She said, "He came over to see Dad."

"Did you talk to him?"

Nan looked up at her brother. "Well, yes, sort of."

He nodded. He needed a shave, but his beard was like 150-grit sandpaper and made him look kind of young and vulnerable. Rocky said, "He's been hankering after you for too long, Nan. What you need to do is set him straight."

She felt her jaw drop. "Is that right?" she squeaked at last.

"Yep. You left in a hurry and without talking to

him. Now, I don't know why you acted like that. Dad said you must have had some powerful reason. I think he thought Davis went out on you, you know, with another girl or something. Maybe he did—I don't know. What I do know is that it left Davis kind of up in the air. He needs a decent ending to this thing, Nancy.''

''What?''

''An ending. He needs to understand why you left 'cause I really don't think he knows. He needs you to tell him you don't care about him, real plain and simple like that, so he can put you behind him and get on with things.''

This was weird. This was more conversation than she'd ever had with Rocky, and, what's more, he was talking as if he knew what he was saying. Nan said, ''Like what? Get on with what things?''

''Like life. You kind of snapped him in two when you left.''

''Get more specific,'' she said slowly. She had the horrible feeling she was about to discover she was responsible for Davis's failure in medical school.

''Well, take girls, for instance. There's this one who likes him a lot. Her name is Greta Walters. You know her?''

''No.'' This wasn't what she'd expected. She'd been surprised Davis wasn't a doctor, but it had never occurred to her to wonder if he was attached to someone else, to another woman. The news hit her hard.

She put the semiclean platter on the table and sat with her hands folded up in the dish towel.

"I guess Greta moved to town after you were gone. She works at the hardware store. Davis is in there so much that they got to be friends, and I happen to know she's crazy about him, but he still thinks he's hung up on you. It's not fair, you know. To Davis, I mean."

"No," Nan said. "It's not fair. But I don't think he's hung up on me, you know. I think he's angry with me, that's all. And I guess I can't really blame him for that."

"Get real, little sister," Rocky said softly. He pulled the plug in the sink, ruffled her hair with a damp hand, and exited the kitchen right as Boris entered.

"I need more iced tea," he said. "Whipping your father at checkers takes it out of me."

Nan, who was still reeling with the revelations of the last five minutes, gestured weakly at the fridge.

After Boris poured his tea, he came to stand beside her.

"I was a doctor for forty years," he said, his eyes bright and curious as he studied Nan's face. "I know shock when I see it."

"Just fatigue," Nan mumbled as she stood.

"Hmm—" he said skeptically. "Listen, Nan, I'm not going to pry into why you left town so suddenly or try to make you feel guilty for not coming back even once in almost five years.''

''Thank you,'' she whispered. She didn't add that he'd said practically the same thing when he picked her up at the bus station just that morning. Obviously he was dying to know what had happened. She sighed deeply. There were so many ramifications to coming home. She'd assumed it would be between her and Kyle Todd. She hadn't figured on fathers, brothers, friends, shopkeepers, old boyfriends, and surrogate uncles.

''Your dad has missed you,'' Boris said. ''You know how sentimental the old fool is.''

Nan touched his cheek. ''Yes,'' she said simply. ''But Dad used to visit me pretty often. You even came with him a time or two, remember? Later this summer, when Dad's leg is healed, why don't the two of you come again?''

''It's better having you here, in Sage, in your father's house,'' Boris persisted. ''You must come back often.''

''Why? Why must I come back often? Why do I have the feeling you're not telling me something?''

''Maybe you have a guilty conscience,'' he said, patting her arm, the twinkle in his eye in full force.

Nan nodded. If there was one thing she had tonight, it was a guilty conscience. ''Dad's leg will be okay, won't it, Boris? He will be able to walk again? He will get better? I don't know what he'd do if he couldn't work at the diner.''

''His leg will be as good as new,'' Boris assured her.

Nan looked into his eyes, searching for the truth. There was no way of telling if she found it or not.

Chapter Three

"Then I'll pick you up around seven," Paul said.

"Fine, fine," Nan said absently. She had been busy scanning the yellow-pages directory when he called, uncertain where to start to find daily help for her father. She looked under Home-Care Agencies—which suggested she try Social Service Organizations—while trying to concentrate on what Paul was saying about dinner.

"—wonderful food. We'll have a great time."

"Yes, sounds nice," she said. There was a listing for something called the Nevada Access Project. Was that right?

"Nan?"

"Anywhere you want," she said. There was also a Senior Resource Service. Her dad was a senior, but she had the feeling he wouldn't appreciate the label. Maybe she should look under Housekeepers.

"How about Chinese food? I know of a great little restaurant in Shanghai, China. Is your passport current? We could leave tonight and be eating steamed dumplings and Peking duck in two days."

"Great," Nan said, sighing deeply. Wait, there was a listing for the Reno Community Action Agency. Certainly they'd be able to refer or advise her.

"Nan?"

"Hmm."

"Nan Hillman, listen to me!"

Nan looked into the receiver. "Paul? What's wrong?"

"You haven't been listening to a word I've said."

"I haven't?"

"No, you haven't."

She closed the telephone book and said, "I'm sorry, I guess I'm a little distracted. Now, then, you want to have dinner."

She was surprised when he laughed. "Yes, I want to have dinner. Is it okay with you to leave the restaurant choice to me?"

"Of course," she said. A car sounded outside. "Listen, Paul, I have to go. I'll see you at eight."

"Wait, Nan. I'm coming at seven, remember?"

"What? Oh, of course. At seven. I'm sorry, but I really do have to go." She hung up and ran through the kitchen. The last she'd looked, Clive had been asleep in a lounge chair situated in the shade between the cottonwood trees. She was glad he was getting some rest and anxious for it not to be interrupted.

Clive was sitting up in the lounge chair as she came through the screen door. Davis Todd was getting a toolbox out of the back of his truck. She paused on the top step and took a deep breath.

One thing was made obvious by the banging in her chest. Seeing Davis again wasn't going to be easier. Her feelings didn't seem to be fading; if anything, they were more intense.

He spied her as he crossed the rocky drive to the cottonwood trees. For a second his gait seemed to slow, but only for a second. He nodded and approached Clive.

Rocky was wrong; he had to be, Nan thought. Davis wasn't still carrying a torch for her. She watched as he sat down on the chair facing the lounge, his back to her. She heard him say, "Afternoon, Clive. I'm ready to start that work in the kitchen."

"Wait a second," Nan said as she crossed the yard. Both men looked up at her as she ground to a halt beside them. "What work in the kitchen?"

"Davis is going to fix those blasted cabinet doors," Clive said as he stretched and smothered a yawn in his fist.

Nan stared at her father, who was suddenly busy contemplating his fingernails. "Those cabinets haven't closed properly for as long as I can remember," she said.

"High time they were fixed, wouldn't you say, Davis?"

"Leave me out of this," he said with a shrug.

"Why do you suddenly want them fixed now, Dad?"

"Why not?"

Nan nodded. She wasn't sure what was going on, but here, in front of Davis, wasn't the time to find out. Instead, she thought a project of some kind was in order, and she said, "Well, it's your kitchen. Anything special you want for dinner?"

"Well, now. Matter of fact, I do have a hankering for tamale pie with lots of them black olives in it. How about you, Davis? You like tamale pie?"

"You know it's one of my favorites."

"Then how about eating with us tonight? Nan's turned into a fine cook. Boris and Rocky say she's better than her old man. How about it?"

Davis looked at Nan. "It sounds fine to me," he said. "If it's okay with Nancy."

"It's okay with her, isn't it, honey?"

Nan said, "Well, of course, but—"

"See, she's happy to have a hungry man to cook for. Aren't you, honey?"

"I don't mind, but—"

" 'Cause I can't be much fun to rustle up a meal

for lately. Just don't seem to have much of an appetite."

Davis, who had been staring at Nan as she tried to tell her father about her dinner date with Paul, said, "Clive, I have a feeling your daughter is trying to say something."

"Thanks, Davis," Nan said. "Yes, I was trying to say something. I was trying to say that I'll be happy to make tamale pie for the two of you, but I won't be here for dinner. I have . . . plans."

"Plans!" Clive sputtered. "What plans?"

"Paul Avery asked me to dinner, and I accepted."

"Well, tell him you unaccept."

"She can't do that," Davis said.

"Why not? She's here to look after me, isn't she?"

"And isn't she?" Davis asked. "Didn't she just ask you what you wanted to eat and volunteer to make it for you?"

"That's not the point," Clive grumbled.

For a moment they were all three quiet, and the only sound came from the river singing on the rocks and the wind playing in the cottonwood leaves. Finally Nan said, "Davis, you will stay and eat with my dad, won't you?"

"Of course."

She nodded and went back into the house.

Nan spent the afternoon on the phone, and by the time three o'clock rolled around, she'd arranged for

three women to come to the house the next day to be
interviewed for temporary housekeeper/cook. None
were able to live at the house, and she had the nagging
worry that her father shouldn't be alone all night.
Maybe Boris could move into one of the empty bed-
rooms for a while.

While she was on the phone, she was constantly
aware of Davis working on the cabinets not more than
five feet from her. Out of the corners of her eyes, she
watched him take off the old cabinet doorknobs and
install new magnetic catches. His hands were sure
and nimble; she wondered why he'd given up medical
school. She also wasn't sure what to say to him. If
Rocky was right, if he did still think he was in love
with her, she should say whatever it was that would
take him off the hook.

But how did you go about asking a man like Davis
Todd if he was still in love with you? Yes or no, the
answer would embarrass them both. She finally got
the idea that if she gave him what he said he wanted—
a plausible reason for why she left, a reason that
would kill any lingering fantasy he had about her,
assuming he did—it might do the trick.

But not here, not in the kitchen, not with her father
liable to waltz—well, hobble—in at any moment.

"I've been thinking," she said as she arranged the
ingredients for tamale pie on the counter.

Davis looked up from drilling new holes in the

cabinet to accept the larger stainless screws. ''Is that right?''

''Yeah. I was thinking about what you said yesterday. Maybe we should talk. I'd like to . . . tell . . . you about what happened. If you still want to know, that is.''

''I still want to know,'' he said.

He was wearing jeans again and a white cotton shirt. He had a silver watch with an intricately inlaid Navajo band on his wrist. The turquoise and onyx pattern caught Nan's attention, and she found herself wondering if he'd bought the band himself or if it had been a present from someone. A woman, for instance. Like Greta Walters perhaps?

''Okay,'' Nan said. ''We'll talk.''

He ran a hand through his dark hair, messing it up a little, doing nothing to detract from his good looks. He studied her for a second and added, ''I'll come by for you early tomorrow afternoon, and we can go for a drive. Your dad usually naps, then, right, so he won't miss you?''

Nan was touched by his thoughtfulness. She said, ''I'll be busy with interviews until two o'clock.''

''I'll come after two.''

She nodded and turned back toward the sink, away from the scrutiny of those deep-blue eyes. He wasn't hers anymore. He hadn't been for almost five years, but it was beginning to feel as it had so long ago when she'd had to leave without a word. She'd chosen to lose him then, and now it felt as though she were making the same choice all over again. She heard him working behind her and didn't know what she was going to do if she had to be in the same room with him another second. Stuffing a can of black olives back into the cupboard, she turned around quickly.

"Is your truck automatic or standard?" she asked.

"It's automatic."

"May I borrow it? I have to run into town for Dad's olives. I'll only be a minute—"

"Of course you can borrow it. The keys are in the ignition. Just be sure you lock the back, because a lot of my tools are in there."

She nodded her thanks and escaped the kitchen, or rather, Davis's presence.

The truck had complained about going up the ravine, but after the landscape flattened out, it gamely traveled the two miles into Sage as if it was on autopilot—a good thing as Nan felt distracted by the Forty-Niners football cap on the passenger seat, the Mozart tape in the cassette player, and the dozens of candy wrappers littering the floor. Years ago Davis had had a fondness for football, classical music, and candy; apparently these passions were still in full flower.

She slowed down when she reached Sage, unsure where to go, what to do. That's when she spied the lopsided sign, once white, now beige, with *Cactus*

Cup painted in letters that looked—kind of—like cacti. She pulled along the curb in front of it, locked the truck, and opened the door.

Her father had bought the Cactus Cup the year Nan's mother died, and in the ensuing sixteen years not much had changed. It was composed of two rooms—dining area and kitchen. The dining area was small, accommodating two window-hugging tables that seated three each and that claimed a view of downtown Sage, and a counter that seated ten more customers who got to look at each other or the cook.

Nan smiled at the host of memories that danced through her mind as she took in the pink Formica counter that made a big U around the diner, the old-fashioned cash register, the vinyl-covered stools, the coffee machine, the big grill, and the ever-troublesome hot-chocolate machine. The linoleum on the floor was still cracked; the picture of a cactus growing out of a coffee cup, which Nan had painted when she was twelve years old, still hung on the wall, and it was still crooked.

Harry was in the process of cleaning up, evident by the wet rag on the counter and the mop leaning against the wall that led into the back room. The diner served only breakfast and lunch. Nan closed the door, and Harry's voice rang out from the back room, where he couldn't see the door.

"Who's there? We're closed! Can't you read the sign?"

Nan looked at the door, where the OPEN side of the sign was still turned toward the street. She said, "Yeah, I can read. That's why I walked on in." She turned the sign to CLOSED.

Harry erupted from the back room, his thin face set in a scowl until he saw Nan.

"Good golly! Nan Hillman, you did come home. How are you, girl, how are you?"

This last question was accompanied by a hearty handshake that threatened to tear Nan's arm from her socket. She smiled, but she kept her mouth closed, afraid the smile might erupt into a rude laugh because Harry Mule looked even funnier than usual.

Harry had always reminded Nan of an aging turkey, with blue eyes, a generous helping of synthetic brown hair perched atop his head, and a set of false teeth that would have done a television game show host proud. Now, without the toupee and with only a few singed hairs for eyebrows, the image was even more complete.

"I'm fine, Harry," Nan said, extricating her hand. She perched on the nearest stool and said, "Don't let me keep you from your work."

"Listen, girl, I ain't cleaned the coffee machine yet. Let me get you a cup." There was no use protesting, as he was already filling a cracked cup that leaked only a little.

"Thanks," Nan said as she put a napkin under the cup to soak up the getaway brew.

Harry watched her and said, "I dropped a few cups yesterday. Thought I caught all the broken ones. Hey, you won't tell your dad, will you? About the cups, I mean."

She smiled. "No, I won't tell." She took a sip of the coffee. It was all she could do not to spit the acrid liquid out of her mouth. She swallowed it and tried smiling, but the aftertaste about killed her.

"Pride myself on my coffee," he said proudly. "Cup of Joe ain't doing its job if it don't raise the hackles on the back of your neck. By golly, it's good to see you, Nan. Good to see you."

"It's good to see you too, Harry," Nan said, but in the back of her mind she wondered how long the meager profit margin at the Cactus Cup would last with Harry at the helm.

Eventually Harry went back to loading the dishwasher, and Nan tried not to hear the crashes and bangs that probably meant her father was going to have to buy more dishes when his leg mended. Unseen, she hopped over the counter, dumped her coffee, and began washing down the counters. She discovered one section was sturdier and a little pinker than the rest and realized this was what Davis must have rebuilt for her father. It looked as though he did good work, but she wondered how he managed to support himself with little jobs like this and the one he was currently performing at her dad's house. More important, she mused, how did a man as intelligent as Davis remain satisfied doing such menial tasks?

"It's none of my business," she told her reflection in the coffee urn and continued washing the tables and mopping the floor. She left as Harry prepared to clean the grill. It was a dirty, sweltering job, and the fan above the grill was so loud, conversation was impossible.

For a few seconds Nan stood on the sidewalk outside the diner. She glanced at her watch, discovered she'd been gone almost an hour, and decided she'd better get back. She was halfway home before she remembered the olives, so she turned around, drove back into Sage, and parked outside the store.

Nan was relieved when she found that Marjorie Block wasn't behind the counter. She paid too much for a can of pitted black olives she didn't need, then toyed around with the idea of peeking into the hardware store, curious about what Greta Walters looked like, but in the end decided not to be so nosy.

While she was crossing the sidewalk to Davis's truck, she happened to look down the block, and what she saw made her freeze in her tracks.

Marjorie Block stood in front of Todd's Pharmacy, her finger extended, looking for all intents and purposes like an aging Irish setter pointing out a pheasant to its gun-toting master. With a sense of shock Nan realized the old man standing next to Marjorie was Kyle Todd.

It was several seconds before Nan could force herself to move again. But when she did, she didn't move toward the truck as she longed to, but down the sidewalk, toward the pharmacy. It was time to start dealing with facts instead of fears, and if her knees felt like overcooked spaghetti noodles, at least they carried her in the right direction.

Kyle wasn't aging as gracefully as Clive or Boris, Nan decided as she drew closer. He'd always looked pinched to Nan, as though his features had frozen in a permanent sneer. The general air of dissatisfaction with life had intensified over the last five years so that while he'd always looked petty, he now looked mean too.

Nan knew he was about fifty-five, but he looked ten years older. His hair was an unflattering shade of pewter, his skin pale and tight over his bones. The only trait he seemed to share with Davis was the sapphire blue of his eyes. On Davis the color hinted at untapped depths; on Kyle it just looked cold.

Marjorie took a step toward Nan. "I was just telling Kyle that I saw you driving Davis's truck," she said, seemingly unaware of the friction between Kyle and Nan. "I was telling him that it's nice you and his son are friends. All that stuff about those drugs is ancient history! I told him, kids will be kids—"

"For heaven's sake, Marjorie!" Kyle barked.

His voice had always reminded Nan of fingernails

scratching the proverbial chalkboard, and she stopped in her tracks.

Marjorie said, "I was just—"

"Why don't you go back to work? I'll call you later."

"But, Kyle—"

"Now!" he snapped. Marjorie glared at him for a second, but in the end she left. Nan was startled by his rudeness, by her acceptance, by the whole pairing in general. If ever there was a more mismatched set of people than Kyle Todd and Marjorie Block, Nan wasn't sure she wanted to know about it.

For a few seconds Kyle and Nan stared at each other. Finally Nan said, "I'd like to talk to you. Let's get off the sidewalk."

He nodded briskly and turned to go inside the store. Nan followed. Like everything else in Sage, the pharmacy didn't appear to have changed in the five years she'd been gone. There was still an old-fashioned soda fountain running along the north wall; shelves with assorted toiletries, greeting cards, and pharmaceutical supplies running fore and aft; a long counter in the back with prescription drugs kept behind that. Two old ceiling fans twirled lazily above with seemingly no effect on the stuffy inside air.

The store was empty, but Nan realized immediately that she was at a disadvantage inside this building. Kyle had always been boss here, and as soon as she stepped over the threshold, she could feel him grow more confident while her own resolve seemed to falter.

"What are you doing back in Sage? More important, what are you doing driving my son's truck?"

"You swore you wouldn't tell anyone about those accusations," Nan countered. "You told Marjorie Block."

"That woman has a big mouth," he grumbled. "But listen here, that doesn't explain what you're doing back in Sage. I thought I told you to stay away."

Who does this man think he is—Marshal Dillon? Nan wondered as she looked at his thin face. She steadied her voice and said, "My father is ill. I'm back only for a few days."

"I know your father broke his leg, but he's got your brother."

"Yeah, well, my brother isn't much good in a kitchen."

He frowned. "Just for a few days?"

"Just a few days," Nan assured him, and then, screwing up her courage, added, "Listen, Mr. Todd, I was pretty young when you and that . . . that man accused me of selling him amphetamines. I was scared. But as I told you then, I didn't do it, and I'm getting kind of tired of hiding from something I didn't do."

"You're forgetting I have proof," he said. "I know you're guilty, so don't bother lying to me again. It didn't work the first time, and it won't work now, either.''

''What kind of proof?'' Nan asked.

''Remember Vince Frisk? He wasn't looking too good the last time you saw him, because you hadn't had a chance to sell him any more of those amphetamines, and he was hurting. Well, I know how to get in touch with him anytime I want because he and Davis were friends once. You remember that. One call and he'll come.''

''Wait a minute. You're telling me that this Vince person and Davis were friends?''

''Maybe not friends. Davis helped him out in school, that's all. Vince was about to flunk some bonehead math class, which meant he'd be kicked off the basketball team, and that was apparently the only reason he bothered going to school. Anyway, Davis tutored him. My son always excelled in mathematics.''

Nan shook her head. It didn't make sense. Why would Vince accuse her of something she didn't do? ''The word of an acknowledged addict,'' she said, ''wouldn't hold much weight—''

''I have written proof. Records, things like that. I had to use some pretty fancy footwork to sidestep the Nevada law, young lady. I went out of my way for you. But the records prove the drugs were missing, and you were the only one who could have taken them—and don't think I won't prosecute just because

I might get in trouble too! Besides, what with Vince's word, I think you'll agree that staying out of Sage is in your own best interest.''

Nan bit at the inside of her bottom lip as she thought. If she hadn't sold those amphetamines, and she hadn't, then who had? To her knowledge, besides Kyle, only she and Davis had worked in the pharmacy that summer.

As she looked closely at Kyle, a thought so awful entered her mind that for a moment she felt dizzy and sick to her stomach. *Davis.* Could Davis have sold the amphetamines to Vince? Kyle had just said Vince was a friend of Davis's. More than a friend, a man who owed another man a favor. Would he protect Davis by lying to Kyle about her? Nan looked into Kyle's eyes, and she saw something shift, something retreat, and it occurred to her that maybe, in the back of his mind, Kyle knew or suspected the same thing Nan did!

''I'll give you until the end of the week,'' Kyle said. ''No more.''

Nan nodded woodenly. She needed to get out of the pharmacy, away from Kyle Todd. She needed time to think.

''And I want you to stay away from my son,'' Kyle added. ''I don't want him consorting with the likes of you. I never did tell him how you used him to get a job at the pharmacy, but don't think I won't!''

Without uttering another word, Nan turned and left.

In all the years she'd had to think about the incident, it had never occurred to her to consider Davis as a suspect. Why not? In fact, she'd never considered anyone else even though she knew she herself was innocent. Had she purposely avoided thinking about that angle of it because inside she was afraid of what she might find?

Somehow she made it to Davis's truck, remembered how to turn the key, how to drive. Somehow she found the right end of town and a few minutes later crawled down the ravine to the river, where Davis sat outside under the cottonwoods, visiting with her father.

Chapter Four

"You look beautiful," Paul said as Nan searched the kitchen for her purse.

"Thank you," she mumbled, suddenly conscious that Davis as well as Paul was looking her over from head to foot and, even worse, that she was more concerned with what Davis thought of her in the two-piece blue rayon dress than what Paul thought.

It had taken her longer than usual to dress, considering all she did was iron out a few wrinkles, fasten a couple of buttons, and pull her hair into a loose French twist, but she'd felt like a leaf caught in a whirlwind, one minute convinced she'd been paying for Davis's mistake for the past five years, the next convinced he'd no more sell drugs illegally than she would.

"I like a woman in a dress, don't you, Davis?" Paul asked.

"Some women," Davis said, which earned him a quick glance from Nan and a chuckle from Clive.

Davis and Clive sat at the table, both of them picking at the tamale pie, their gazes split between Nan and Paul. Nan sighed with relief when she found the beige leather bag hooked onto the back of the chair in the corner. At last they could get out of the house, where the tension was so thick it practically clouded the air.

"Don't be too late," Clive said.

Nan wanted to tell him that she was a little old for him to start treating her as if she was going out on her first date, but one look at the dark circles under his eyes stilled her tongue. "I won't," she said softly. "You go on to bed when you're tired. I'll see you in the morning."

"I'll wait up for you," he said.

Paul cleared his throat. "Actually, Clive, we might be late. We're going into Reno to an exclusive little club I know of. They serve a sole almondine you wouldn't believe."

"Nan doesn't like fish," Clive said.

Paul looked at Nan. She smiled briefly, withheld the scowl she felt like throwing at her contrary father, and said, "I'll see you tomorrow, Dad. You too, Davis."

He nodded. His fork was buried in his dinner, his

face set in an expression Nan couldn't begin to read. Weary with the moribund attitude in the house, she opened the screen. "Come on, Paul. It's a beautiful night."

And it was. The wind was soft and warm; the desert looked as though it were lit from within, and the early-evening shadows were long across the river. Nan got into Paul's car and for the first few miles let the music on the radio soothe her jangled nerves. She tried to empty her mind of her newfound suspicions about Davis, tried not to wonder why her father had acted so crazy in front of Paul. It was good to be away from the house with a companion considerate enough not to chatter.

"So what did you mean that you'd see Davis later? I thought he was in the past."

"Well—"

"Because he's trouble. I mean it, Nan. You've been away. He's changed. He even tried to get my wife to sneak around behind my back."

"You're kidding!"

"Of course, Alison turned him down. I'm only telling you this so you'll know to stay away from him. I don't think you should see him, do you?"

Nan met Paul's gaze, which she held until he had to look back at the road. She took a deep breath.

"Try not to take this the wrong way, but I think we should get something straight right from the start," she said. "You and I were casual friends once, more because of Alison than because we had much in common. I'm really glad you asked me to come out with you tonight, and I'm sure we're going to have a nice time, but please, don't forget that my private life is my private life, and I don't want to discuss it with you. I'm sorry if that sounds rude, but that's the way it has to be.''

He glanced back at her. At last he said, ''Okay. I apologize for prying. I was just surprised to see him eating at your table. I was under the impression you didn't have much use for him. I know he and your dad have been getting friendly over the last year or so, but—''

''Paul? Can we just drop it? Let's talk about something else. It looks as though we're going to have a gorgeous sunset tonight, doesn't it? I'd almost forgotten how big the sky looks without trees or fog to block it—on the Oregon coast, the sun just seems to plunge into the ocean.''

He followed her lead, and they talked about the weather for a while, then a string of other inconsequential things. Nan was feeling comfortable again by the time they rolled into Reno, the self-proclaimed ''Biggest Little City in the World.''

The club Paul mentioned was on the outskirts of town, away from the brightly lit casinos. Nan ordered the sole almondine just to spite her father and ate every bite. The ambience was low-keyed, the clientele looked like local business people, the service was slow but pleasant. After they ate, Paul insisted they stop by one of the casinos, and Nan plugged a handful of nickels into a progressive poker machine while Paul did the same, only with silver dollars.

For Nan, gambling had always been the one drawback of living so close to Reno. She didn't care for the glassy-eyed way some people got as they played two machines at once, their attention off somewhere as their hands pulled down on the handles, which would either mean their coins would be swallowed forever, or a few more would be spit out. It was all electronic now; in fact, the arms were just for show. One could simply push a series of buttons. Most of the machines didn't even pay out winnings until the player pushed the right button directing it to do so.

Nan wandered around the casino alone because Paul was on a winning streak. She declined several offers for a free drink and yearned for a breath of clean air. She finally took a seat behind another nickel machine because her feet hurt, and when the cocktail waitress asked what she'd like, she ordered a tomato juice on the rocks.

She heard Rocky's voice and turned around just as her brother's hand clamped down on her shoulder.

"Little sister, what in the heck are you doing here? I didn't know you gambled."

She smiled up at him. "I'm a real daredevil. I bet I've lost thirty-five cents so far."

As he laughed, he moved a bit, and Nan realized

the lovely woman standing beside Rocky was actually with him. She was a delicate blonde in her early twenties, with straight shoulder-length hair, peridot eyes, and a charming sprinkle of light freckles across her nose. She was wearing beautifully tailored jeans and a white blouse, but it was her jewelry that caught Nan's attention. Strands of liquid silver glittered around her neck, a concho belt wrapped her waist, and a ring of silver, turquoise, and red coral all but covered one slender hand.

Rocky saw Nan staring. "This is Greta Walters. Greta works at the hardware store. This is my baby sister, Nan Hillman."

The two women shook hands briefly. Greta said, "Rocky has told me all about you."

Nan darted a look at Rocky, wondering what he had told Greta, and he winked at her. She realized with some chagrin that she didn't know her brother well enough to decipher the wink.

"He told me about you too," Nan said.

"He did? Really?" Greta looked up at Rocky and added, "What did you tell her, Rocky?"

"That you were my friend," he said simply, a faint blush spreading up his neck. This won him another dazzling smile that seemed to pierce his soul, and Nan began to understand. Even though she didn't know her brother as well as she would have liked, it was obvious that he was crazy about Greta Walters, who was apparently crazy about Davis Todd.

If Nan was reading things correctly, Rocky wanted Davis free of any lingering romantic inclinations toward Nan so that Greta could have a shot at him. If Rocky was selfless, then he was doing it for Greta's sake. If he was as in love with her as Nan suspected, he was doing it because he hoped Davis wouldn't be interested in Greta and then she might open her eyes and see Rocky.

But how could Davis not melt under the lime-green gaze of the tantalizing Greta?

Paul chose this moment to reappear. He was smiling big, which, Nan assumed, meant he'd won big. He offered to buy everyone a drink, but it turned out Rocky and Greta were on their way to meet one of Greta's friends and couldn't stay. Nan declined too, tired of thinking and supposing. She longed for the cool Oregon coast, even for the rowdy sixth-graders who were getting ready to graduate to junior high school with a substitute teacher because Nan was busy in Sage making a mess of things.

"I want to go home," she told Paul. "Do you mind?"

"No problem," he said.

They were back beside the river in no time. Davis's truck was gone, but the house was ablaze with lights. Paul parked in a dark area of the driveway and came around to open Nan's door. When he helped her out of the car, he kept her hand and tucked it up under his chin; then he bent to kiss her.

Nan went ahead and returned the kiss. It must have meant more to him than it did to her because he initiated another one. She pulled away gently and slipped her hand from his.

"Thank you for a lovely evening," she said politely. The truth was, she was glad it was over. It had been a strain to keep the conversation going on the way home—she suspected that wasn't Paul's fault but her own, for she had seldom, if ever, gone out on a date with one man while consumed with thoughts of another.

"I want to see you again," Paul said.

There was no overhead moon, and the house lights didn't reach into the shadows, so Nan tried to put the smile into her voice in case Paul couldn't see her face. "It's a very tiny town. I'm sure we'll run into each other—"

"No, not like that. Like this. In the dark, under the stars. I want to hold you again—"

"Paul, really. We hardly know each other. Besides, I'm very busy, and I won't be here long."

"You're not too busy to see Davis again."

Nan said, "I told you once this evening—"

"I know, I know. I'm sorry. I know I'm assuming too much, but I've been lonely since Alison died and, seeing you again . . . well, it makes me feel like there might be a chance to get back something I've lost."

Nan swallowed her discomfort because of the pain she could hear in Paul's voice. "I'm sorry," she said.

''I hope you find love again, I sincerely do, but, Paul, pinning your hopes on me when we hardly know each other seems like a mistake.''

She felt his hand on her arm. ''What's there to know?'' he asked. ''I've always been attracted to you, Nan. Remember, I even asked you out several times, but you always said no.''

''Alison always liked you,'' Nan said, remembering. ''I wouldn't have hurt her for the world.''

''Is that why you wouldn't date me, because Alison liked me?''

''That's why,'' she said, not sure if it was the only reason or not. Truth of the matter was, she hardly remembered Paul.

He laughed softly. ''Well, I'll be!''

Nan took a step away. ''Thanks for dinner.''

''Tomorrow night?''

''No, like I said, I'm just here for a few days.''

''Long enough for Davis—''

''Paul!''

She heard him sigh deeply. At last he said, ''After you left Sage, I got the job at the pharmacy you abandoned. Did you know that?''

''I had no idea.''

''Well, I'd helped out there for years, but that summer I'd gone to work with my dad in his insurance office, and so you got the job. When Kyle needed part-time help again after . . . after you left, I did that too. Actually, I'd been helping out now and again all along, just when you or Davis weren't available.''

Nan thought back five years. She'd completely forgotten Paul used to be in and out of the pharmacy all the time. Even now, his presence there seemed shadowy—probably, she realized, because the only person who had seemed real that summer had been Davis. She touched Paul's sleeve. ''Where is all this going?'' she asked.

He sighed again. ''I saw Davis after you left. He was broken, Nan, really torn apart. If he's after you now, it's probably because he's still thinking about you from then. Have you considered that?''

''Yes.'' She wished with all her heart that everyone would stop telling her how much she'd hurt Davis.

''Just think about it, will you? And when you come to your senses, give me a call?''

''Good night, Paul.'' Nan waited until his taillights had disappeared up the road, and then she sighed deeply. Why couldn't everyone fall in love with the right person? Why did people seem to want someone they couldn't have? She went inside, roused her father from his chair, then took herself off to bed and a night of uneasy dreams.

Beth Robins was a tiny little woman barely out of her teens, with tight little curls and a bow-shaped mouth. Nan felt like a giant standing next to her, and even though she asked her all sorts of questions, she never seriously entertained the idea of hiring the eighty-eight pounder. For one thing, the woman looked as though she'd crumble like a buttercup beneath the heel of a logger if Clive ever fell and needed help getting up.

After Beth left, Nan scrubbed the walls in the kitchen, getting them ready for a fresh coat of white paint. She was standing on a ladder, attacking the ceiling with Spic and Span when the second interviewee arrived.

If size alone was all that mattered, this woman could have played linebacker for any of the top five National Football League teams. She moved her bulk around awkwardly, breathing heavily from the exertion of walking from one room to the other, and Nan wondered if she'd have the stamina for an eight-hour-a-day job, one that required some major housekeeping along with cooking. She needn't have worried, as the woman was so distraught over the absence of air-conditioning that she told Nan she couldn't possibly consider the position.

Nan was on the ladder again when she heard a third car arrive. As she opened the screen door, a smile spread across her face.

"JoJo!" she screeched and, dropping her cleaning rag, ran across the yard.

The older woman folded Nan in a motherly embrace. Nan eventually tore herself away from JoJo's arms and looked at the face that she'd loved for so many of her formative years.

JoJo was fifty-eight, a statuesque woman whose hair was grayer than it had been; in fact, it now matched her eyes, which had always seemed especially deep to Nan, eyes that traveled way back into the soul. They perched above a generous nose and a mobile mouth that broke into wide smiles at the drop of a hat.

"After I got things running smoothly here, I was going to come see you," Nan said.

"Of course you were," JoJo said. "About time you came home."

Nan nodded and listened yet again to the opinion that she had left too abruptly, been gone too long, and owed it to her father not to behave in this manner again. There was no way to tell JoJo—or anyone else, for that matter—that that was exactly what she was going to have to do within a few days unless she could figure something else out, and as she could hardly disagree, she took it with her chin high and prayed for it to be over soon.

"You've got that exact same expression you used to get on your face when you'd come into the store after school and buy junk food and I'd tell you how bad it was for you and try to get you to eat a piece of fruit," JoJo said at last. "I give up! Where's your dad?"

"Over here under the trees," Clive called out,

"listening to you lecture my daughter. Won't do you any good. The girl is pigheaded."

"Just like her old man," JoJo said as she took Nan's hand and the two of them joined Clive in the shade.

"Did you come all the way over here just to insult me?" he asked.

"Mostly. How's that cast holding up? Looks pretty good, but you haven't had anyone sign it yet. Hey, what are you doing out here in the noonday sun, anyway? You should be inside in front of a fan."

"Ah, Nan's interviewing baby-sitters for me. And she's cleaning. Got the whole place smelling like disinfectant."

"Maybe she should go on down and disinfect that diner of yours. I bet Harry Mule has more food on the floor than he does in the pans. If the Board of Health visits while that man is at the helm—"

As JoJo spoke words of gloom, Nan found herself drifting into a fantasy she'd harbored since she was eight years old: JoJo and her father married, living here in this house together, taking care of her and Rocky and Steven. When she'd been a kid, this had been her most cherished dream, and now, looking at the two of them sitting side by side on the lounge, she wondered anew why they never had married.

She came back to the present in time to hear JoJo tell them she was having an informal barbecue the next night, insisting they both come.

"I never turn down food," Clive said, and Nan looked at him closely. The tamale-pie leftovers proved that her dad wasn't up to his usual appetite. For that matter, the amount of leftover food proved that neither he nor Davis had felt much like eating the night before, or maybe all it proved was that she'd been so upset by her run-in with Kyle Todd that she'd left some key ingredient out and the stuff tasted like cardboard.

"What was wrong with dinner last night?" she asked him. "You didn't eat much."

"Too much chili powder. Even Davis noticed. Just ask him."

"I wasn't grilling you, Dad. It's just that you don't seem to like my cooking."

"Oh, your cooking is fine," Clive said slowly. "It's my appetite that's off. I told you that."

"Hmm—"

"I bet she cooks better than that Harry Mule," JoJo said. "I had lunch there today. His special of the day was meat loaf, and it tasted like he put sugar in the mixture. Lots of sugar. It was awful."

"He's going to kill my business!" Clive lamented.

Nan took it upon herself to get the topic of conversation away from Harry's incompetence. "I'd love to come to your barbecue, JoJo. Dad told me you bought a new place."

"You'll love it. I've got animals coming out of my

ears, and I take care of them all myself except for the cows, which your brother likes to feed and milk.''

''Rocky?''

''You're surprised, aren't you? Well, Rocky is a rather surprising young man. He's great with livestock. Hey, I think I'll ask Davis too.'' Nan nodded stiffly and JoJo added, ''Time was when that news would have put a smile on that pretty face of yours, Nan darling.''

''Well, that was a long time ago.''

''I got the boy coming over tomorrow to fix that windowsill in the kitchen,'' Clive said with a sidelong look at Nan that reminded her that this was the second time he'd employed Davis to do menial chores that had been ignored for twenty years, right when Nan would be stuck in the same room.

Obviously there was some kind of plan afoot. Nan had no delusions that Davis had anything to do with it; she suspected he was as innocent of this minor-league plotting as she was. She said, ''That'll work out well because I think I'll spend tomorrow outside getting the house ready to paint. Which reminds me— we've got to find someone to paint it for you, Dad. It looks kind of shabby.''

• ''The house?'' he asked, bewildered. ''Do you really think so?''

Nan looked at JoJo. ''What do you think?''

JoJo shook her short hair. ''It looks old and ignored, but what do I know? I look old and ignored too. Besides, I have a barbecue to worry about.''

Nan, making her voice as neutral as possible, said, ''Do you think you'll ask Davis's father too?''

''That sourpuss—why should I?''

''Oh, you shouldn't, you shouldn't,'' Nan said. Then, noticing the speculation in both sets of gray eyes, she added, ''I mean, you should if you want, but you shouldn't if you . . . don't. You know what I mean.''

''Hmm—'' JoJo said.

Nan was saved from further questions when the third interviewee showed up and she was able to leave JoJo and her father to entertain each other.

Nan felt like Goldilocks in the fairy tale. The first bear's bed was too hard, the second, too soft, the third, just right. Well, the first housekeeper had been too small, the second, too big, but this one, May Calhoun, was fine, just fine. She was a comfortable-looking woman with a cheerful smile. She didn't smoke, didn't drink, liked housework, and had met Clive at the diner.

''I can take care of the old dear,'' Mrs. Calhoun said, even though Nan's father wasn't much more than ten years older than Mrs. Calhoun herself.

''I'm sure you can, Mrs. Calhoun,'' Nan agreed. ''It's important . . . important to me, anyway, that Dad eat well. You do cook?''

''Mercy me, child! Do I cook? I'll make him real

rib-sticking food—you watch. There isn't a man been born that won't eat my chicken and dumplings. That's what Mr. Calhoun, God rest his soul, used to say. Leave the old gentleman to me.''

Nan had never heard her father described that way before; maybe it would keep him on his good behavior if she told him what Mrs. Calhoun said about him.

Mrs. Calhoun said she'd report for work the day after tomorrow, a handshake ensued, and the friendly woman was on her way.

After she left, Nan started to join her father and JoJo again, but when she saw them sitting close, their heads bent together as though they were deep in conversation about something private, she retreated into the house.

She made it no further than the kitchen table, where she plopped onto one of the chairs, stretched out her legs, and took a deep breath. At last she'd accomplished something. If Mrs. Calhoun came to work in two days, Nan could leave in three, maybe four days.

Her father had a doctor's appointment in Reno the day after tomorrow, and though he protested, Nan had every intention of going to that appointment with him. By then she could have a new coat of bright paint on the kitchen walls, if she painted at night when Davis wasn't around, and maybe her father would agree to having the house painted as well. Rocky might know someone who needed a job; for that matter, maybe Rocky would take the hint and do it himself. That reminded her that she needed to talk to Boris about staying nights for a while.

Nan put her head down on her folded arms and closed her eyes. In three or four days she'd be gone from here. She was ready to put Sage behind her, ready to get on with her life and forget about Kyle Todd for good. A horn honking reminded her that there was still one more hurdle to conquer before she could escape. She looked out the window in time to see Davis getting out of his truck, here to take her on a drive so she could attempt to tell him why she'd left so abruptly.

With a healthy jolt of stage fright, Nan realized this meant she had about five minutes to think of something good, because if there was one thing she wasn't prepared to tell him, it was the truth. Or was she? She honestly didn't know.

"We used to drive around like this a lot," Davis said as he took a narrow track out into the desert. It couldn't really be called a road as it consisted of no more than tire tracks, but they looked well used, and the ride wasn't too bumpy. A Mozart tape played softly on the cassette player and the Forty-Niners cap swung from the rearview mirror, but the candy wrappers were gone.

Nan smiled to herself. They had driven a lot that summer because it had been the one way they could be assured of being alone. Was Davis remembering the easy kisses they'd shared while stretched out on the hood of his truck, a slightly older version of the model he drove now? Was he remembering the vast sky above, full of stars and hopes and dreams, or the words they'd exchanged, the forever they'd promised? She glanced at his profile and felt pretty sure he wasn't harboring any romantic memories at that moment. He looked as though he were concentrating on something. His eyes were narrowed; his forehead was furrowed.

He was different, she realized. He'd been fun loving and laugh-prone that summer, full of games and jokes. This man was quieter, more closed in, more careful. Was she to blame for that?

"What happened to medical school?" she asked.

"It didn't work out."

"I know. Why didn't it work out?"

He sighed deeply. "What's it matter?"

"I thought the past always mattered."

He looked at her. "I said that, didn't I?"

"I believe so, yes. So what happened?"

"I thought we were going to talk about you. More specifically, I thought *you* were going to talk about you."

Nan looked out her window. She saw that the track was ending in a modest wooden house that appeared empty. A large unattached garage loomed up behind the house. The yard was composed of scrub and sagebrush; big buckets of sun-hardy flowers ringed the half-circle drive and a path to the door. Davis pulled the truck up beside one of the buckets and killed the engine. He sat back against the seat.

"Medical school didn't work out because I didn't want it to work out. Truth of the matter is, I never wanted to be a doctor. There, that's all you need to know about that."

"Then why did you work so hard to get into medical school?" Nan persisted.

Davis hooked his arms over the steering wheel, another gesture Nan remembered. She also remembered the way his hair touched the top of his ears, the way his profile looked as though it belonged on the front of a coin. Her gaze followed his arms and landed on the unfamiliar watchband that glinted bright silver in the afternoon sun.

At last he said, "I tried so hard because of my father." He followed these simple words with a steely blue gaze that pinned Nan to the seat. "He wanted me to be a doctor. I did everything I could to let him know how little I wanted it. Everything short of actually telling him in plain English, that is. I didn't want to hurt him, so I did a lot of stupid, spiteful things, hoping he'd get the message, only he never did, and now we don't even talk." He ran one hand through his hair and added, "Okay, Nancy, I've spilled my guts. I expect you to do the same."

Nan nodded because her tongue seemed to be tied in some fancy knot. In an attempt to be spiteful, had

Davis sold those amphetamines to Vince Frisk? Was his father supposed to find out about it and refuse to send Davis on to medical school? Had Davis spent five years thinking the whole matter had been undiscovered? But what about Vince? Wouldn't Vince have told Davis what happened?

"It's too hot to sit in the truck," Davis said. "You look as though you're ready to faint."

He got out of the truck and came around to open Nan's door while she worked on untwisting her tongue. He took her hand as she stepped outside, but he dropped it immediately. Nan mumbled, "Where are we?"

"My place."

Nan looked again at the orange-and-yellow flowers, at the charming house painted brick-red, and the huge garage towering behind it, and then she looked at Davis. "Yours?"

"Mine. I built it myself. In fact, it's really not finished yet. The house is empty inside; it's just a box with a stained exterior."

"Then where do you live?"

"In the workshop for now. Come on, I'll show you."

She followed him up the path to what she'd assumed was a garage but which Davis called a workshop. The building was one-and-a-half stories high with few windows, finished with the same wood and stained exterior as the house. Huge double doors faced the house, but Davis chose a small door to the side and opened it for Nan. He flipped on a switch, and the dark interior came to life.

Nan would have been hard-pressed to name many of the tools that confronted her. What she saw was a large floor space with long benches and orderly rows of hand tools lining the walls. Four huge ceiling fans descended from the high ceiling; a black cast-iron stove looked ready for a winter day. In the middle of the room was another long table, and here and there were individual machines that reminded Nan of the ones on the cartoon shows, the ones that were used to threaten little mice and sailors and innocent maidens. Everywhere, there was lumber—stacks of the stuff. Some of it was dark, some light, some golden, some brown. The wood accounted for the smell, she decided—rich, aromatic, almost heady. And off to one side of the room was the most beautiful trunk Nan had ever seen.

''Did you make that?'' she asked as she approached it. The trunk was about three feet long and two feet high and glowed reddish brown. There was scrollwork on the sides, intricate corners that showed how the wood was joined together, a mirrorlike finish that begged the human hand to touch. Nan touched it. It felt like glass; in fact, she could see her reflection on the surface of the lid. She'd never seen any piece of furniture half as beautiful.

''It's lovely,'' she said, feeling her words were

inadequate. No wonder her dad had been so annoyed when he thought she was putting down Davis's vocation.

"Thank you," he said. "It's a hope chest. I guess that's old-fashioned. I guess it should be called a blanket chest, but Greta keeps calling it a hope chest, and I got in the habit."

"Greta Walters?"

"You know her?"

"Slightly."

"Oh. Well, yes, I made it for Greta."

"I see," Nan said. She looked away from the box, her infatuation with its beauty tempered a little. She saw several other boxes in various states of construction on one of the tables. These were much smaller than Greta's hope chest, but the same craftsmanship was obvious. One in particular caught Nan's eye. It was about the size of a small toaster, and the joints were so smooth, it almost looked as though it had been carved out of a single piece of wood. Small drawers lined with deep-blue velvet rolled in and out with polished ease.

"The box is made out of African mahogany," Davis said. "Do you like it?"

"Very much. It reminds me of a little box in my father's room that I admired yesterday when I changed the sheets on his bed. Did you make that too?"

"As a matter of fact, I did. I gave it to him on his last birthday."

"You're really quite good. Do you make anything besides boxes?"

He smiled for the first time that day, and to Nan it felt as though the sun had suddenly peeked from behind a rain cloud. "Not at first I didn't. For some reason I seemed compelled to make boxes, one right after the other. Your father asked me if I was boxing something in or boxing something out."

"What did you tell him?"

"That I just liked making boxes. However, I am trying to branch out a little now. I made a table and six dining-room chairs last year for a woman in town. It took forever."

"And was it as satisfying building the table and chairs as it was building a box like the one you built for Greta?"

His smile suggested he was looking inside for the answer. When he spoke, his voice was subdued. "No, as a matter of fact, it wasn't."

Nan nodded and stared at his hands. A doctor's hands, Kyle had always bragged to anyone who would listen. Or a craftsman's hands. Gentle, sensitive fingers that could turn a piece of wood into a box that needed no glamorous filling to be dubbed a treasure chest. She swallowed hard, overcome with a variety of emotions.

"Would you like something cold to drink before you tell me what happened five years ago?" he asked.

She'd almost managed to forget about that! She set the box down and said, ''Sure.''

She watched him walk to an old refrigerator in one corner. There was a hot plate on an overturned crate, a cot made up with a lightweight sleeping bag, a reading lamp, and a shelf of what appeared to be well-read books. While he produced a pitcher of something icy green from the refrigerator and searched for glasses, which he finally produced out of another box, Nan rehearsed what she was going to say:

I left because I didn't love you anymore, and I was too chicken to tell you so. I left because I was young and selfish and didn't want to face the truth. I left because I was afraid you'd try to talk me into staying and I knew I didn't want you to.

There wasn't a word of truth in it, but what were her options? She could tell him she left because his father threatened to prosecute her if she didn't. If Davis was guilty of selling Vince those drugs, he would then discover what he'd put her through. She knew he'd be consumed with guilt and for what reason? He had rebuilt his life; he was obviously in love with Greta Walters; what would she accomplish by telling him what had really happened?

Or he would be startled by her claim because he had no idea any drugs had ever disappeared out of the pharmacy because his father had managed to convince Vince to keep his mouth shut. This would mean someone else stole the drugs—maybe Vince all by himself or someone Nan didn't know. At any rate, Davis would be furious with his father for threatening Nan, which would serve what purpose? Already alienated from each other, it could well mean the end of any chance of a relationship between the two. Did she want to be responsible for that?

And what would Kyle do when Davis confronted him with Nan's story? If he could be believed, and Nan thought that he could, he'd prosecute her, and if she was lucky, all that would happen would be that she'd lose her job in Oregon. All for what? So that Davis wouldn't hate her for leaving and she could come back to live in a town she didn't want to live in, anyway?

She watched him come back across the workshop, a glass in each hand. She watched him set the glasses on the long table and then drag two stools over. She watched him with longing because she realized she'd lost him, really lost him, and she didn't like it.

"Maybe this wasn't such a good idea," she said.

"Oh, no, you don't," Davis said. "You're not backing out now."

"I don't want to hurt you—"

"The time when what you said could hurt me is past," he said softly. "Now all I want is to understand."

She nodded. "I know. Like I said before, we were young. I was only eighteen."

"And I was twenty-three, but I wore my heart on my sleeve like a little kid."

"You don't anymore."

"No, I don't anymore. All it takes is one good break, and a man's heart learns to stay behind a bit of cover."

"Davis—"

"Don't feel sorry for me," he interrupted. He took a long swallow of the lime juice in his glass, wiped his mouth with the back of his hand, and met Nan's gaze. "Just tell me, Nancy. I've been wondering about it for five long years. No, don't get to feeling guilty. I know you were a kid, and I bet I even know why you left. I just want to hear it from your lips."

"You know why I left?" she gasped.

He studied his hands. When he spoke, his voice was low and soft, and Nan had to lean forward to hear him. "I was older than you," he said slowly. 'I was frustrated with the educational goals my father had set for me, but I wasn't strong enough to tell him. And then I met you and you came to work at the pharmacy, and suddenly the frustration vanished. Because of you, I thought.

"I also began to think that I would stay in Sage and ask you to marry me. This is the tricky part, Nancy. We both heard the rumors around town, that we were getting married, and I always laughed at them just like you did. I think you knew somewhere inside you that I wasn't really laughing, and it scared you because, although you loved me, you didn't love me in the same intense, almost desperate way that I loved you. I think you picked up on my intentions, didn't know how to handle them, and ran.''

Nan hadn't breathed while he spoke. She expelled her breath, willing Davis to look at her. Finally she stood, took his hands into hers, and squeezed them. He looked up, and for a moment their eyes locked, and it was as though the intervening five years hadn't happened.

Nan found herself in his arms. At first they were unyielding, shocked, but that lasted only a fraction of a second, and then his lips were on hers, his hands wrapped around her back, crushing her in an embrace that seemed to hold her together. He ran his hands up toward her neck, catching her hair in his fingers, his lips trailing over her eyes, down her cheek. . . .

''Nancy,'' he whispered.

At the sound of his voice reality reasserted itself. Nan swallowed hard and pushed herself gently away. He released his hold of her, and unsteadily she sat back down on the stool. This time it was she who was afraid to raise her eyes.

For a long time neither one of them said a word. Nan was about to address what Davis had said when the stillness was shattered with a telephone ring.

He stood abruptly, but he didn't move to answer the phone.

''Hadn't you better get it?'' she asked.

He shrugged broad shoulders, as though a ringing phone were the least of his worries, but it kept up to the point where he finally grabbed the receiver and barked, ''Yes?''

Nan saw the tense knot in his jaw loosen as he listened to a voice she could hear was female. He said, ''No, you weren't interrupting anything.''

She bit at her lip as Davis listened. When he spoke again, he said, ''No, of course I have time to talk with you. This evening would be fine. I'll pick you up around six, all right? No, don't worry about it, I understand. Okay, good-bye.''

He put the receiver back and sighed. ''Greta Walters,'' he said, gesturing unnecessarily at the phone.

Nan nodded. ''I'm sorry I threw myself at you,'' she said quietly. ''I don't know what came over me.''

''Don't you?''

''I honestly don't, unless I just got caught up in the past there for a moment. What you said before that? Well, you were right. I was just out for a . . . a good time . . . but you wanted more, and I . . . I didn't know how to handle it all properly. I bolted. It was wrong to leave like I did.'' She looked at him out of the corners of her eyes. Did he believe her?

He took a deep breath and stared at the cement floor. ''I thought as much,'' he said at last. ''Only problem with that explanation is that it doesn't explain your pathological reluctance to return to Sage, does it?'' He looked up and caught her staring at him.

She hadn't thought of that. She shrugged. "I guess I just didn't want to run into you again."

She thought he looked unconvinced, but at last he put out his hand. "Okay, but all that's behind us now. We've each gone on with our lives. Let's shake hands and come out friends."

Nan put her hand in his, ignoring all the little shocks that raced up and down her back. "Friends," she said.

He glanced at his Navajo watch and said, "I guess I'd better get you back to the house before your father sends out the Marines."

It wasn't until they were almost back to her dad's place that she asked Davis where he'd gotten the beautiful watchband. "Greta found it for me," he said.

It didn't surprise her one bit.

Chapter Five

T he winter had been a dry one, and summer had come early. These two facts conspired to heat up the afternoon and bake the weeds Nan was trying to pull into ropy string that refused to budge from the hard earth. She'd already asked her father for a sickle, a hoe, a shovel—anything! He claimed to have no tools, but he was so clearly annoyed that she had insisted on working outside, cleaning up the foundation of the house so it could be painted, that she didn't know whether to believe him or not.

No matter, she decided as she yanked on a handful of dry, golden grass. She was not going to paint the kitchen while Davis worked on the windowsill, and that was that. Riding back in the truck the night before had been bad enough.

How had this happened? she wondered as she sank to her knees to tackle the weeds closer to the ground. She'd gotten over Davis Todd years before. Oh, sure, she'd cried her heart out every night for a year, but that was long over. She'd even dated a few times and entertained the thought of maybe falling in love again someday. But all that was back in Oregon, back where the sun was gentle and the fog persistent.

It had been awful watching Davis drive away the day before, knowing he was on his way to Greta's house. It had been awful opening the door this morning and finding him on the step, toolbox in hand, a soft smile on his beautiful lips. Neither of these things was as awful as the afternoon before, when he'd told her he'd been thinking of staying in Sage and asking her to marry him five years ago and she'd agreed that fear of that very thing was what had driven her away.

Truth of the matter was, she'd had no idea he'd felt that strongly. She'd thought hers was the wild, desperate love, that he had so much school ahead of him that he'd never wait for her. It had never occurred to her that he'd abandon his dreams for her.

Wait a moment. Not his dreams . . . Kyle's dreams. She'd had no inkling of his unhappiness over that, either, which was beginning to make her think she'd been a pretty unperceptive teenager back then. Or maybe she'd just been so in love that the details had escaped her.

Oh, what did it matter? she decided as the weeds

finally relinquished their hold on the gritty soil. She moved on to the next patch and realized she was jealous. Jealous of Greta, because it appeared Greta was going to get what Nan had been too stupid to stay and fight for, namely Davis Todd.

That's when she remembered the barbecue at JoJo's house that night. Davis had supposedly been asked. Nan put her chin in her hand and thought for a moment—perhaps tonight she'd talk to him again. Perhaps tonight she'd find out if he was really in love with Greta, or if perhaps he still harbored feelings for her, because the more than obvious truth of the matter was that she still harbored lots of feelings for him.

The kiss yesterday proved that something still existed between them, didn't it? She thought of the feel of his lips on hers, the thrill of his hands tangled in her hair, caressing her back, the sound of his voice as he whispered her name. . . .

Nan didn't realize a smile formed on her lips, nor did she realize it drooped as the logical next conclusion occurred to her. What good would it do if Davis was in love with her or if he could possibly love her again? There was Kyle Todd to think about, and he'd made it quite clear he wasn't going to tolerate any involvement between Nan and Davis even if father and son were currently alienated from each other.

The whole thing was hopeless.

* * *

"Dad, I can't drive you over to JoJo's place, because I don't know how to drive your stick shift."

"That's ridiculous," he huffed. "I taught you myself."

"No, you taught Steven and Rocky, but you never taught me. You said it wasn't ladylike. That's what's ridiculous."

"I would have taught you if you'd stayed in Sage instead of running off when you were still a kid," he muttered as he searched through the papers on the table for the cordless phone. "We'll have to get Rocky to take us on over."

"Rocky is going too?"

"Everyone is going. JoJo throws a swell party."

Nan listened to her father convince her brother to come give them a ride to the barbecue. She wasn't sure her dad was up to an outing like this one—he was still popping pills, and he wasn't eating much to speak of. In fact, she could see a weight loss in the few short days she'd been in Sage. On the other hand, he'd been getting along without her nursing for five years, and he'd have to again in two days, so she held her tongue. Maybe she would talk to his doctor about it the next afternoon. This reminded her that if she couldn't drive stick shift, how was she going to drive Clive into Reno? She'd have to borrow a car.

"What happened between you and Davis yesterday?" Clive asked as they waited for Rocky.

Nan looked down at her hands. "Nothing."

"Oh, I see. You came home looking like you were going to break into tears, he comes over here today and barely speaks a word while you spend the day out in the sun, pulling those stupid weeds no one cares about—but nothing happened between you. Is that right?"

She swiftly glanced at him, then away. "More or less."

"You two are both muleheaded!"

Nan nodded. "I know. I also know you're trying to get us together, Dad. Give it up; it isn't going to happen. He's no more anxious to spend time alone with me than I am to spend time alone with him. I'm sorry things didn't work out the way you wanted, but—"

"Rocky's coming," Clive interrupted, hefting himself to his feet with the help of the crutches. Nan took the hint and dropped the subject.

JoJo's ranch was five miles out of town. It turned out she owned several acres of rolling brown hills and the ubiquitous sagebrush. She also owned three big dogs and two small ones, numerous cats and chickens, a few cows, and one big black horse, and it seemed to Nan that all of them were there at the barbecue either underfoot, in lap, or peering over a fence.

There were also about thirty-five people in attendance. Nan saw that JoJo had set up a comfortable-looking chair right smack in the middle of the festivities on which she ensconced Clive. Rocky went in search of Greta, and Nan tried to appear as though she weren't looking for Davis.

"He'll be here," JoJo said softly, coming up behind Nan.

Startled, Nan laughed. "I don't know what you mean—"

"Oh, honey, you may be able to fool yourself, but you can't fool an old geezer like me."

Nan shrugged. "Listen, I was wondering if you have a car I could borrow to take Dad to the doctor tomorrow afternoon."

The older woman frowned. "Isn't Boris going to take him?"

"That's the plan, but I have to go home in a couple of days, and I'd feel better if I talked to the doctor myself."

"Does your father know about this?"

"I told him I wanted to come."

"And what did he say?"

"Not much. Something like, 'We'll see.' But you know Dad—he thinks I'm eighteen years old."

JoJo nodded. She was carrying a striped tabby, and a small black dog sat on one of her boots. At last she said, "I think you should let Boris drive your father."

"Why?" Nan demanded. "What's the big deal about going to an orthopedist's office?"

"Nothing, honey. That's not the point."

"Then what is the point?"

"Like you said, you're not going to be here to see your father through this ordeal, and Boris is. They have a system worked out. I'd leave it alone if I were you."

"But he's my father, and I'm worried about him. Have you noticed the way he's losing weight? He doesn't seem to have much of an appetite, and he's tired so much of the time—"

"Then why are you leaving him again?" JoJo interrupted. "Your school year is almost over up in Oregon, right? Why don't you call up there and have them extend your substitute teacher and stay here and take care of your father?"

Nan was shocked by the anger she could hear in JoJo's voice. She blinked back tears and shook her head, speechless.

JoJo said, "I'm sorry, Nan. I guess I love the old coot too, and I hate to see you leave again."

"He can come north to see me as soon as he's out of the cast," Nan mumbled. "I asked Boris if he'd come too. Maybe Dad could get Harry Mule to run the diner and stay several weeks. Maybe you could help me talk him into it. Would you, JoJo?"

With her free hand, JoJo touched Nan's arm. "We'll see," she said gently, her gray eyes as deep as Nan had ever seen them. Then suddenly they left Nan's face, and a smile spread over her mouth. "Look who's here," she said. "Not that you care."

Nan turned around and bumped into Davis.

He was wearing blue jeans and a black cotton shirt. He steadied Nan with warm hands that lingered a moment on her arms, effectively robbing her of any ability to make conversation.

"Glad you could make it, Davis," JoJo greeted him.

"I wouldn't miss one of your parties," Davis said as he let go of Nan and kissed JoJo on the cheek.

"I see you brought Greta along. How nice!"

Nan looked over Davis's shoulder in time to see Greta climb out of his truck. She was wearing a jeans skirt and a pale-yellow blouse. Nan looked down at her own white jeans and the sleeveless orange T-shirt she'd worn and wondered why it hadn't occurred to her to dress up a little. She hated feeling jealous of another woman—it was a new and disquieting experience—and she forced herself to extend a warm smile as Greta joined the group.

"Good to see you again," Greta told Nan. She looked around the crowd and added, "Did Rocky come?"

"He's over visiting with the cows," JoJo said, gesturing toward the barn.

"He likes animals," Greta said. She cast Davis a perturbed look and added, "I'll see you in a while," then walked off toward the barn.

Nan wondered what tale of woe Greta was going to spin for Rocky. Was the woman blind? Couldn't she see how Rocky felt about her and stop using him to complain about Davis?

Boris came up behind JoJo. "You want me to supervise the barbecue?" he asked.

"Would you?" she said, smiling up into his eyes. She turned back to Davis and added, "Why don't you introduce Nan to Lightning?"

"Sure," he said. He touched Nan's arm. "Come along, you've got someone special to meet."

Nan didn't want to be alone with Davis, and she hesitated. He smiled and leaned down to speak in her ear. "You can't hide from me forever, you know."

"I haven't been hiding—"

"Yes, you have. I thought we shook hands and came out friends."

"We did," Nan said.

"Good. Come on."

Lightning turned out to be about a ton of black horse with two sable-brown eyes. "He's a gelding," Davis said as he put his hands around Nan's waist and hoisted her onto the top rung of the fence. He sat down beside her, and they patted the huge black head that nuzzled their hands and snorted onto their legs. Nan had never been that close to a horse before, but this huge, gentle creature didn't seem much like a "Lightning" to her, and she told Davis so.

"He came with the name. To hear JoJo tell it, he never runs if he can walk, and he eats his weight in hay every other day. She got him to ride around her land, and she says that although he's not the most exciting mount in town, she loves him, anyway.''

Lightning put his warm, soft muzzle against Nan's cheek. ''I can see why,'' she said.

''They love him too,'' Davis added, pointing out the two big dogs that were camped out around the horse's feet.

''Doesn't he ever step on them?''

''Sometimes. He broke Duke's foot—that's the shepherd mix—last year. Accidentally, of course. But JoJo plastered it up, and a couple of months later he was as good as new.''

''She's really something, isn't she?'' Nan asked as she gripped the fence. Lightning's affections were getting a little rambunctious, and she was in danger of being spilled onto the ground.

''Knock it off, Lightning. JoJo? Yeah, she really is. Have you ever wondered why she and your father never got together? It's obvious they love each other.''

Nan nodded slowly. Davis was looking right into her eyes, and she made herself return his intense stare. ''Sometimes love isn't enough,'' she said as Lightning nibbled on her knee with his lips.

''Don't you think it should be?''

''It isn't always that easy.''

''Why?'' he demanded. ''Two people who love each other belong together, don't they?''

''I don't know . . .'' she said.

He sighed and rubbed the horse's ears. "I've been thinking about what happened yesterday."

This is what Nan had feared would happen. She tried playing dumb and said, "What happened? We finally had that talk, and we patched things up—"

"And we kissed."

She met his eyes briefly. "Yes," she said, almost breathless.

"Was it really just a mistake—a sentimental journey, if you will, into the past?"

For several seconds Nan stared at the horse; then she finally raised her gaze to Davis. She stared into his deep-blue eyes and wondered what he wanted out of her, what the point to this conversation was. She opened her mouth to speak, to tell him that she wasn't sure what the kiss had meant, when she glanced over his shoulder and noticed Rocky and Greta emerging from the barn. Rocky was looking down at the ground, but Greta was staring at Davis's back. Nan saw Greta tell Rocky something; then she veered away from him and began jogging toward the fence.

Nan let herself back down onto the ground. "I smell something good cooking," she blurted. "I'll see you later."

His hand touched her shoulder, and he said, "You can't go yet. You haven't answered me."

"The kiss was a mistake," she said softly and left.

* * *

Nan slept restlessly. It seemed as though she spent half the night reviewing the conversation she'd had with JoJo about Clive, and the other half reliving the conversation with Davis about love and marriage. Since neither conversation could be labeled satisfying, it made for interrupted slumber.

She awoke early—it was still dark outside. For a moment she thought another dream had startled her into wakefulness; then she heard a thump on the ground and realized it was coming from her father's room. She waited, wondering if he was okay and if she should go check on him; then she heard the unmistakable sound of his door squeaking open, and she waited for the peculiar noise he made as he manipulated the crutches through the living room. It didn't come. Curious, Nan got up, pulled on a robe, and went to investigate. The lights were on in the kitchen.

He was standing in front of the open refrigerator, peering inside. His crutches were against the table, and he had one arm over the refrigerator door. When he heard Nan, he jerked, obviously startled.

"Don't you think you should use the crutches to support your weight instead of that old door?" Nan asked.

He took the crutches she offered. "Darn things make my armpits sore," he confessed.

"I didn't hear you use them to get from your room to the kitchen. Do you think it's wise to put any weight at all on your foot?"

"I didn't," he grumbled as he slammed the door.

Nan smiled. "Why are you up so early? May I make you something to eat?"

He sat down on a chair. "JoJo tells me you're leaving day after tomorrow," he said.

She sat down opposite him. "I have to get back to my class, Dad. I talked to Rocky last night, and he promised me he'd get your house painted. Mrs. Calhoun comes tomorrow and—"

"You've got my life all arranged, don't you?" he interrupted.

"It wasn't my intention to 'arrange' your life. You called me and said you needed help for a few days, and that's what I've tried to do. Dad, why are you up so early?"

"Got to go into the diner."

Nan's eyes flew open. "What? You can't be serious."

"Fired Harry Mule last night. He showed up at JoJo's party. Do you know why the meat loaf tasted so sweet? Because he dumped a jar of wheat germ flavored with brown sugar and honey, that's why. And do you know what the special was he had planned for today? Spam crepes. Nan, I shudder to think what that man will do to a crepe, and since when does the Cactus Cup serve Spam? But that's not all—he said he was going to jazz it up with Cheez Whiz!" He shook his head and added, "You should've heard people talking about the Cactus Cup when they thought I wasn't listening. The place is becoming a joke.''

"But, Dad—"

"Got to go in, that's all there is to it. Got to get the place back on its feet before I lose it. Now, Nan, I know I asked you to come, and I know I've seemed uncooperative since you've been here, but I want you to know I truly appreciate what you've done for me. Years ago you had to do what you had to do whether or not anyone else understood. I supported you, didn't I? Now I have to do what I have to do. I wouldn't go if I didn't have to, but there just isn't anyone else.''

"There's me," she said softly.

"You're leaving."

"No, Dad. I'll call Oregon and arrange everything.''

"I can't have you do that."

"And I can't have you standing in the diner all morning. There's no other way, and you know it, so don't fight me.''

"But, Nan—"

"And when you and I and Boris drive into Reno this afternoon for your doctor's appointment, we can stop by a store and pick up supplies. The appointment is at four o'clock, right? Plenty of time to do breakfast and lunch, clean up, and prepare for tomorrow before we leave.''

"Nan, dadgumit—"

"I'd better get dressed and get into the diner. You still turn on the grill first thing?"

He stared hard at her, his eyes narrow slits in his weathered face. "It's a toss-up," he said at last, "between turning on the grill and starting the coffee. Just don't put your head down by the pilot light. Hate to see you lose your eyebrows and all that coppery hair."

"I'll be careful. And don't forget, Mrs. Calhoun comes today. Be nice to her."

Clive snorted, and Nan decided Mrs. Calhoun was on her own.

Nan had spent more summer vacations than she cared to count helping her father at the Cactus Cup, and as she opened the door and switched on the light, a host of memories swamped her. This was different, though. This was for real. Her dad wasn't going to be hovering over the grill cooking; she was. She was going to be doing the dishes, cooking the lunch special, making the coffee. A flutter of nerves tickled her insides.

Well, she told herself sternly, *if you can get up at five and walk two miles into town because you still don't know how to drive that blankety-blank stick shift, then you can darn well cook a few breakfasts and make a couple of lunches.* At least she wouldn't have to spend the day outside, escaping a close encounter with Davis. At least here she'd be free from her meddling father.

Hungry customers began arriving at six o'clock, and from then until eleven, Nan was so busy frying hash browns, flipping pancakes, buttering toast, pouring countless cups of coffee, and folding omelettes, she didn't have time to worry about how she was going to handle the daily lunch special. In an odd quiet moment, she searched the big refrigerators in the back and found a stack of crepes Harry had obviously prepared the day before. She heated one on the grill and tasted it. Not bad, she decided. Maybe she could come up with something that could utilize the crepes.

Meanwhile everyone in town seemed to realize she and not Harry Mule was at the diner, and everyone in town seemed to think it his responsibility to stop by, ask her why she'd been gone for so long, and tell her how nice it was to have her back. While Nan was flattered, she was also uneasy. What would happen when Kyle learned she was still in town? What would happen when she didn't leave at the end of the week as promised?

She found three big bunches of spinach in the fridge. She was alone in the diner, busily blanching the spinach while stirring a white sauce in preparation for spinach and cheese crepes when the door opened and Davis walked in. He was carrying his toolbox.

He did a double take when he saw Nan behind the counter. "What are you doing here?" he asked. "Where's Harry?"

Nan took the saucepan off the burner. "Dad fired Harry," she said as she approached the counter. "What are you doing here?"

"When did he fire Harry?"

"Last night."

"Why?"

"Something to do with sweetened wheat germ and meat loaf and Spam. What are you doing here, Davis?"

He sat down on the stool by the cash register. "Guess who decided the rest of the counter needed work?"

"Dad sent you over?"

"Called me and said it couldn't wait."

"I sense a pattern."

He frowned. "What do you mean?"

"First he hires you to work at the house when he knows I'll be there, and now he's got you over here because this is where I am."

"You think he's trying to throw us together?"

"It seems likely."

"He's never said a word to me."

"Nor to me."

"Maybe it's all coincidence."

"I don't believe in coincidence."

"But he couldn't know he was going to fire Harry."

"But once he did, all he had to do was reroute you," Nan said.

As they talked, Nan poured him a cup of coffee

because all morning long she'd been pouring coffee for anyone who sat down. He took a sip and smiled. "Better than Harry's and your father's, but don't tell them I said that."

She nodded slowly. The diner was warm, and her cheeks were flushed from the heat of the grill. She could feel her long hair escaping the loose ponytail she'd caught it in at the beginning of the day, and, looking down at her white apron, she found evidence of the morning's work. She wanted to be clean and sparkling for Davis, wished she were wearing a white dress with lace—

What was she thinking of! She shook her head.

"Is something wrong?" Davis asked.

Everything is wrong, Nan yearned to cry. In an instant, in her mind, she was back in Davis's arms in his workshop, or sitting on the fence with him while a black horse blew on her leg, or driving down a desert trail in the truck cab with him less than a foot from her side, and she realized with a sinking heart that the memories she was going to have to rebury after this endless summer was over were going to be fresh memories, not the slightly dusty, slightly cob-webbed memories of five years before. She was going to have to go through the process of grieving over a lost love all over again, and it was almost more than she could bear.

"Nancy? Are you crying? What's wrong?"

She hastily wiped the tears from her eyes. "It's smoky in here," she said.

"And smoke got in your eyes, like in the old song? But wasn't that a love song?" he mused, and a look of such tenderness stole over his face that she had to look away.

"I don't remember," she said at last. "Well, now that we know what plot my fiendish father is trying to hatch, there's no need for you to stay and fix the counter, is there?"

"The counter needs fixing, Nancy, and a job is a job, so I'm staying. Is that a problem?"

"Of course not," she said and went back to her congealing white sauce and the spinach that was by now hopelessly overcooked.

"Harry couldn't cook like this," Boris said. He'd come into lunch ostensibly to reassure Nan that he would be taking Clive into Reno to see the orthopedist, but Nan suspected the real reason was that he'd been ordered to make a full report to Clive about Nan's debut as chief cook and bottle washer at the Cactus Cup.

She looked at all the other diners, a surprising number of whom were actually eating the special and seemingly enjoying it. Wonder of wonders.

"I'm going with you to the doctor's office," Nan said.

Boris was in the process of chewing. He finished,

wiped his mouth politely with a paper napkin, and said, "Sorry, Nan, but Clive's doctor moved his appointment up to twelve-thirty. Boy, I'd better get going, hadn't I?"

"What kind of doctor sees patients during the noon hour?" Nan demanded.

Boris put a few dollars beside his plate. "A doctor on a diet? I don't know, dear girl. I only chauffeur."

"But I had supplies to buy, and you know I can't drive Dad's old van."

Boris shrugged his massive shoulders. "I'm sorry. Wait, how about Davis?"

"Did I hear my name mentioned?" Davis asked. He was in the process of tearing out a fourth of the counter.

Nan found it incredible that he was working like this while the customers were in the diner and even more amazing that no one seemed to mind.

"You can take the girl into Reno for supplies, can't you?" Boris said.

"As a matter of fact, I do have to go in later. You're welcome to come along, Nancy."

"I don't—" Nan began, but Boris waved her protest away with a flash of his hand.

"Great! Clive will be relieved that's taken care of."

"Wait a second," Nan whispered as she leaned across the counter. "Boris, is this just another of my father's not-so-subtle methods of forcing Davis and me to spend time together?"

"You're a suspicious child."

"I have cause to be suspicious."

"Just don't get paranoid. It is just a happy coincidence that you need to get to Reno late this afternoon and Davis is going along and has room to tote you."

For the second time that day she said, "I don't believe in coincidence."

"Call it what you will, just don't worry about Clive's dinner. I'll treat the old boy to a hamburger and stay at the house playing checkers until you get back."

"I won't be that late," Nan said, frowning.

"Never can tell," Boris replied with a broad wink.

"And Mrs. Calhoun is supposed to be making him dinner."

"Mrs. Calhoun isn't exactly at the house," Boris said, a nervous smile on his lips.

"What!"

"It's a long story, and I really do have to run. See you tonight, Nan. And thanks, Davis."

"No problem," Davis told him, looking up from his job. Nan would have chased Boris down the street and demanded more of an explanation if at that moment the three men at the corner table hadn't decided that they'd try "the fancy special." Nan sighed heavily and went back to work, but from time to time she'd find herself wondering what had happened to Mrs. Calhoun.

It was well after four by the time Nan had boiled

the potatoes for the next day's hash browns, cleaned the floor, counters, dishes, and grill, cleared the cash register, and made a list of all she needed to buy at the store. Davis was measuring and making his own list of supplies as Nan locked the front door. "Ready?" he asked.

"Ready," she told him, mentally preparing herself for another memory in the making.

The road was smooth, the afternoon warm. Davis listened to Beethoven, the Forty-Niners hat pulled down low on his forehead. He had his left elbow stuck halfway out the open window while his fingers curled around the steering wheel. With his right hand he ate an Almond Joy.

"That was a good lunch you made today," he said.

Nan got the feeling he was as anxious to make light conversation as she was. "Thanks."

"What are you going to do, stay in town and run the diner all summer?"

"I don't know." She thought of the call to her principal and the assurances that with only six days of school left, Nan should take care of her father and return next fall. She was not to worry; Mrs. Pilsner would take care of everything.

Not to worry. There was still the not-so-little matter of Kyle to consider. All day Nan had expected the elder Todd to march into the Cactus Cup and demand an explanation, and all day she'd tried to figure out what she'd say. The thought had occurred to her that with Davis in residence, Kyle might stay away, and if so, hurrah for decrepit counters and manipulating fathers.

Or would Kyle just call his attorney?

"Nancy? Do you realize that half the time I ask you a question, you answer with a word or two and then drift off into some daydream?"

Nan blinked a couple of times. "Do I?"

"Yes. So what are you going to do about the diner?"

"I told you, I just don't know!" she snapped. She looked at him, expecting a surly frown, and instead found him grinning. "What are you so happy about?"

"That's the first time you've snarled at me since you got home. Don't you remember? You used to snarl and snap on a regular basis. I kind of liked it."

"I didn't snarl and snap," she snarled. She laughed at herself and added, "I don't know how you tolerated me. I must have been insufferable."

"You were a delight," he said softly, his eyes focused on the road ahead. "Well, here we are—beautiful Reno. I'll drop you off at the grocery store and go on to the lumber supply. I'll be about an hour."

"That's fine," Nan said. She got out of the truck and walked into the store, determined not to look back to see if Davis was staring at her as she longed to stare at him.

Once inside and confronted with a list that seemed

to have no end, Nan concentrated on the job at hand. She bought huge cans of tomato sauce (Thursday special of the day—spaghetti), sixty pounds of potatoes (Friday special—scalloped potatoes with ham), bacon, ham, ground beef, chicken, and cube steaks. Eggs were delivered along with several fresh vegetables, coffee, dairy products, bread and bakery products, so she concentrated on the special items. By the time she made it to the cash register, she found an hour and a half had passed. By the time everything was rung up and bagged, two hours had expired.

She pushed one cart outside while a bag girl pushed a second. She found Davis sitting on the tailgate of his truck, munching on a Mars bar.

"Sorry it took me so long," she said. "You're going to rot all your teeth out of your head, eating all that candy."

"I brush three times a day," he replied and, taking the cart from the bag girl, proceeded to carefully fit thirteen bags of groceries into the truck, alongside several two by fours, five sacks of nails, some metal things Nan supposed were used for bracing, and a length of pink Formica. They were just closing the back when a now familiar voice rang out.

"Davis, Nan, how are you?"

Greta had just driven up. She got out of her car, and Nan internally groaned. Greta was wearing pristine-white shorts and a matching halter top, her hair caught in a lacy bow at the nape of her neck. It was a little discouraging to constantly run into someone who was always as well turned out as Greta was.

"Fancy seeing you guys here. Are you alone?"

"What do you mean?" Nan asked.

"Oh, you know, it's just the two of you? I thought maybe Rocky came—"

"Nope. He's working at the garage in Sage this week," Nan said. "I think he's rebuilding someone's engine."

Greta put her hand on Davis's arm, leaned close, and whispered something in his ear that brought a smile to his lips. He nodded, and then they both looked at Nan.

"Sorry, Nan," Greta said. "I know it's rude to tell secrets. Well, I'd better get my shopping done. Nice to see you two."

"Nice to see you," Nan returned insincerely. She got into the truck and rolled down her window.

They drove for a while in silence. Nan worked on blotting out the image of Greta whispering into Davis's ear and the look of uncomplicated joy that spread over his face. How could a man not love Greta? Nan stopped thinking of herself and started thinking about the agony that must be racing through poor Rocky's heart.

"We were having an interesting conversation last night before you chickened out and left," Davis said as he turned off the freeway.

"What road is this?"

"A little shortcut. It cuts over to the river road. I thought you might enjoy the scenic route. You didn't answer me again."

"What's to answer? I was hungry last night, that's all. No big deal."

"Good. So, now we can continue our conversation."

"I thought we got it straight that that ill-conceived kiss was just a mistake," Nan said.

"I was thinking about what we were talking about before that. Don't you think a man and a woman in love belong together?"

"I said last night that it's not always that easy. Sometimes there are other people to consider."

"That's a point."

A few miles passed, and Nan asked, "Why are you talking about love and marriage so much?"

He shrugged and drummed his fingers on the steering wheel. "I've been thinking about marrying. I want to make sure."

"Oh." She didn't say anything else, and she prayed he wouldn't, either.

Just as he opened his mouth, perhaps to continue the conversation, the truck began making very funny noises. If this was the answer to her prayers, Nan had a feeling she'd made a big mistake.

"Oh, great!" Davis moaned as he pulled to the side of the road and stopped the truck.

"What's wrong?"

"I don't know. Wood, I know, but engines are a mystery."

They stared at each other a moment. Finally Nan said, "We've passed exactly three cars since we pulled off the freeway onto the scenic route."

"I was just thinking that very thing. I guess I'll look under the hood."

She nodded. She gazed out at the rolling hills as he lifted the hood and realized with a start that it felt good to be home in Nevada. She no longer missed the redwood trees or the beaches of Oregon and wondered if she ever had really loved it as much as she professed to or if it was the sanctuary she loved, the sense that she was safe from Kyle Todd and the problems the man posed.

It was no good thinking like this. Oregon was home now; it had to be.

"Nancy? Slide on over and start the engine," Davis called out.

She did as directed, but the engine didn't respond to the turned key and depressed accelerator.

Davis slammed the hood and walked around to the window. He wiped his hand on a rag, took off the Forty-Niners hat, which he tossed into the truck, and said, "I think I made things worse."

"It looks like it," Nan said, and though she knew she should be upset or worried or at least concerned, all she felt was happy that they were stuck out in the middle of nowhere together, which was crazy as she'd spent most of the last two days trying to stay away from him. She tried not to smile but apparently failed as Davis touched her cheek.

"What are you smirking about?"

"Nothing really."

"I hope not. I mean, before you find it too amusing that I managed to get us into this predicament, I should remind you about all that meat you bought, which is even now sitting in the stuffy back of this truck."

"You're right. On the other hand, what good is it going to do me to get all excited about it?"

"Not much."

"I saw a stack of newspapers back there."

"I use them to put down when I stain or paint."

"May I use them to wrap the meat in? Most of it's frozen, and if I wrap it well, it might stay that way."

"Good idea," he said, and together they wrapped all the perishables in several layers of newsprint.

"I could hike back to the road and hitchhike to a service station," Davis offered.

It was getting dark. "How far back to the road is it?" Nan asked.

"About five or six miles. You can come too, if you don't want to be left alone."

She sat on the tailgate. "Do you have a flashlight?"

"Of course not."

"I wouldn't want to get stuck between here and the freeway without even a flashlight. Don't you think another car will be along pretty soon?"

"Seems likely."

"So let's wait."

Davis sat down on the tailgate next to Nan. Together they watched the sunset, and then gradually the sky filled with stars, a virtual avalanche of them.

"I'm getting hungry," Davis said at last. "Maybe we should have hiked. Is there a moon due out eventually?"

"I don't believe so."

"We're not exactly the wilderness family, are we? Well, maybe there's another candy bar in the glove compartment."

Nan laughed.

"What's so funny?"

"You. There's a whole truckload of food right here. Can you start a fire?"

"I think so. I know there are matches in the glove compartment and some scraps of lumber in the back. What do you have in mind?"

"Roasted hot dogs? The Monday special is going to be beans and franks."

"Sounds good," Davis said.

An hour later they sat on the tailgate again, sharing blackened franks off branches of scrub brush, an open bottle of apple juice, and a tepid three-pound can of pork and beans between them. They took turns eating the beans with the only utensil Davis could find in his truck, a putty knife. The wide blade was almost as efficient as a spoon.

"This is nice," Davis said, gazing upward at the brilliant sky.

"Yes. I've missed the desert."

"Is that all you've missed, Nancy?"

She looked at him. His face was half lit by the fire that was quickly burning down to embers. Deciding that on this one night she'd be as truthful as she could, she said, "No, that's not all I've missed."

"Did you miss me?" he asked.

"Yes."

He sighed. "Well, that's something, anyway. Tell me what your life is like in Oregon."

"I thought you said you knew all about me."

He tossed the empty stick aside and leaned back against the Formica. "I know what you're doing out there, but I don't know who you've become. Do you like teaching?"

"Yes." She threw her stick onto the dying fire and wrapped her arms around her knees. "I love the kids. Not all of them, of course, but almost all of them. They're so bright and eager to learn even if they pretend they're bored with the whole thing. It's a challenge to find out who they are, you know, and what they want out of life and to figure out if there's some small thing I can give them to help them find it.''

''You must be a wonderful teacher.''

''So tell me about the wood.''

He smiled. ''Well, there's wood and then there's wood. The stuff I'm doing for your dad is handyman work—almost anyone could do it. That helps make a payment or two, but what really does it for me is the wood I make into boxes. It's kind of the same thing you were talking about. It's like there's a secret locked in each piece of wood and I get to find out what it is. I know that sounds mystical, but I don't mean it that way. It's tangible, you know. And I like working with my hands, always have.''

''Your father said you had the hands of a doctor.''

''My father. Well, we all know he transferred his dreams onto me, and I almost bought into it. If it hadn't been for you, I might have plowed ahead and become a doctor and hated my life and not known why.''

Nan furrowed her brow. ''Because of me?''

''You kind of woke me up that summer. You were pretty and vibrant and sassy. That's JoJo's word, sassy. She uses it to describe one of her cats, and I think it fits you too.''

Nan took a deep breath, smothered her own feelings of lost love, and said, ''I hope if you decide to go ahead and marry Greta that the two of you are very happy. She's lovely, as you no doubt know, and I

only want you to have the best. . . ." Nan's words
trailed off because Davis was laughing.

"What's so funny?" she demanded.

He eventually stopped. He wiped the tears out of
his eyes with his fingers and looked at Nan. "I don't
love Greta."

"You don't?"

"Of course not. She's a nice girl and we're friends
and everything, but I don't love her. I've never even
entertained the thought of loving her or anyone else,
for that matter, not in many years."

"You made her a hope chest!"

"She paid me an arm and a leg to make that chest."

"And your watch—"

"I admired her Indian jewelry and asked her to find
me a watchband, which she did. By the way, I paid
an arm and a leg for the band."

"But she loves you, Davis—"

"No, no, she doesn't love me."

"But she does," she persisted. "I can tell."

Davis cracked a grin. "Now, this sounds interesting. How can you tell?"

"The way she looks at you. The way she shows
up whenever you do."

The grin widened. "Is that right?"

"That's right, and it isn't funny. At least it can't
be to her, so wipe that awful grin off your face."

"Well, well."

"Well, well what?"

"Could it possibly be— No, impossible."

"Davis!"

"Could you possibly be jealous of Greta?"

"Of course not. Don't be stupid."

He nodded. "I don't know what got into me. But I still don't think she's in love with me. Actually, I think she's in love with your brother."

"Rocky?"

"Of course. That's what she whispered in my ear back in Reno. Oh, not that she loved Rocky, but she made some crack about him and his cars. I don't think women make cracks like that about men they don't care about, do you?"

Nan shook her head. "I haven't the slightest idea. Rocky thinks that Greta is in love with you and that you're still— Well, that doesn't matter. If Greta loves Rocky, why doesn't she tell him?"

"Because it's possible that Greta herself doesn't know how she feels. Haven't you noticed the way she's always asking about him, searching for him with her eyes?"

"Rocky doesn't have a clue."

"He's so darned shy, he refuses to even consider the fact that a woman like Greta could find a guy like him so fascinating. Come to think of it, it is hard to believe, isn't it?"

"As a matter of fact, it is," Nan agreed. "I wonder why Rocky doesn't just tell her how he feels?"

"A wise person once told me, it isn't always that easy."

"Touché. I wish I could be sure that she isn't head over heels for you. I mean, Rocky is so certain—"

"Poor sap."

"She's always around you, you know."

"I knew I detected a note of jealousy in your voice!"

"Dreamer," Nan said and, scrambling down from the gate, put away the leftover food.

Davis yawned. "I think we're stuck out here for the night. A car will probably come along in the morning, but I think it's hopeless tonight."

Nan had to agree. He dug around in the back of the truck and came up with an old blanket and an old jeans jacket. He walked out into the desert just beyond the fire, cleared a spot with the side of his boot, and laid the blanket out on the ground.

"I don't think it's too lumpy," he said. He came back to Nan and picked up the jacket, which he insisted she put on. "It gets cold outside, you know."

"I know."

He studied her a moment and added, "If that kiss hadn't been just a mistake! If you'd actually thrown yourself into my arms because you were unable to resist me, then we could keep each other warm tonight."

"Pity," Nan said, the longing in his voice making the pit of her stomach feel like the inside of an erupting volcano. She added, "I was thinking one of us should sleep in the cab."

"Spoilsport."

Nan laughed, which served as a great tension reliever. "What's gotten into you, Davis Todd?" she asked.

"The stars," he said, gesturing toward the wide sky. "Let's sleep out under the stars."

Nan looked at his face, half lit by the dying fire, half dark. Finally she said, "Davis, who are you thinking of marrying if not Greta?"

"Isn't it obvious?"

"No."

"You asked what had gotten into me," he said, standing very close to her. "The real answer is you, Nancy Hillman. I told you the other day that you couldn't hurt me, that all I wanted was the truth, but the moment I found you in my arms, I knew everything I'd said was an out-and-out lie, that no woman has ever been able to hurt me like you, nor has one been able to send my heart into orbit the way you can.

"Tonight—the broken truck, the burned hot dogs, the sky, the opportunity to be with you without distractions and with our past settled—seems like a slice of time out of time, a little piece of desert magic. And just for the record, I know when a kiss is a mistake, and the other day, that kiss, that was no mistake."

She felt his hands touch her face, cup her chin. She felt his lips touch her mouth so gently, it almost broke her heart.

"Maybe you'd better sleep in the cab, after all," he whispered against her lips.

Nan nodded, overwhelmed with his words and his kiss. One thought resurfaced, and she whispered, "Do you mind if I ask you a question? It's been troubling me—"

"You can ask me anything," he interrupted.

"Davis, did you make a pass at Paul's wife?"

"Alison Avery?" he asked as he distanced his face from hers by a good six inches and slid his hands down to hold hers. "Well, let's see. I did some work at their place a couple of years ago, and she followed me around like a puppy. She was a nice woman, but I've already told you that I haven't been making passes at anyone, let alone a married woman. Where in the world did you get the idea I'd do something like that?"

"From her husband."

"Oh."

"Why do you say 'Oh,' like that?"

He shrugged and ran his thumbs along her fingers. "I don't much like Paul Avery. No good reason, really. Maybe it harkens back to that summer when we all three worked at my father's pharmacy and he was always so smug. Besides, I caught him looking at you a few times, and I was young and hot-blooded enough to let it get to me. Back to Alison—I wonder if she told him I'd come on to her so he'd get jealous and pay her a little attention.''

Nan shrugged. It seemed like a strange thing to do, but Nan hadn't know Alison the grown-up, just Alison the kid.

''Nancy?'' Davis said.

She looked up into his eyes. ''Yes?''

''Would it be all right if I made a pass at you?''

''You already made a pass at me,'' she whispered, but the next thing she knew, he'd raised her hand to his lips and was kissing her fingers; then he leaned down and found her lips, and this time the kiss was one hundred percent more of everything a kiss should be. This kiss made an announcement of sorts. It outlined new rules, declared the past over, and demanded a future. Nan lost herself in his arms, but eventually she pulled away.

''We'd better get some sleep,'' she mumbled.

He protested, but Nan persisted, determined to get away from the allure of his hands and lips and give herself the opportunity to think.

It was cool inside the truck; in fact, it was a little too cool, but maybe that was good, as it tended to take her mind off that series of inflammable kisses. Did Davis mean what she thought he meant? Could he possibly still be in love with her to the point of thinking of asking her to marry him? She pulled his jacket close and buttoned it, inhaling deeply to see if she could detect the faint aroma of some exotic wood. She tucked her legs up under her and thought about everything he'd said and not said.

Even the thought of him made her lips curl into a smile. She was almost sure of it—he loved her. What a miracle! She leaned her head back against the window and tried to get comfortable, but it was impossible because the armrest poked into her side. She stretched out on the seat, but it was too short, and her head kind of fell down toward the door. She scooted across behind the steering wheel and peered out into the night, wondering if Davis was having as much trouble settling down as she was, but she couldn't see anything.

With her forehead against the window, she thought. Even if he was still in love with her, what was she going to do about it? Kyle would never stand still while his precious son became engaged to a woman he believed broke the law—which raised a question Nan had been ignoring for quite a while. Could Davis have possibly stolen those amphetamines and sold them to Vince? What would he do if she just point-blank asked him? And if he said no, then what? What had changed in the last few hours that made any chance of a relationship between her and Davis more of a possibility than it had been five years before? Nothing, she realized with a sinking heart. Absolutely nothing.

Davis had said that the past was settled between

them. If he only knew! Still, a part of her heart sang with the knowledge that he might love her, because there wasn't a doubt in her mind that she loved him. On that thought, she fell asleep.

Chapter Six

"We've got to figure out a way to get Rocky and Greta together," Nan told Davis. They were riding in Davis's truck, which was being pulled behind a big white truck. The fact that the truck—complete with a towing bar and a driver who was willing to help out—had happened along right as the sun peeked over the hill made Nan suspect she had a guardian angel looking out for her. This was good, she decided, as she definitely needed all the help she could get.

"Good luck," Davis said dryly.

"How can you be so heartless?"

"I have my own problems," he said as his hand covered hers. She looked at their joined hands, a battle waging in her mind. Somehow she had to discover the truth of the incident that had been haunting her for so long. It was one thing to run away from a man you loved when you were eighteen; it was an entirely different matter now. Now she knew that this was it, her chance for happiness. She'd squandered that chance once; she wouldn't waste it a second time.

"You got quiet on me," Davis said.

"I was thinking."

"I know, about Rocky and Greta. Do you really believe she thinks she's in love with me?"

"I really do."

"I got to wondering about it last night. There I was, lying out in the desert, with a galaxy of stars watching over me, sweet, cool night air blowing across my face, a warm, scratchy blanket under my head, and I couldn't sleep. I have you to thank for that, by the way. Anyway, I got to wondering if Greta thinks she's in love with me because I'm safe."

Nan narrowed her eyes. "Safe" was one of the last words in the dictionary she'd use to describe Davis Todd. "You lost me," she said.

"Safe. Unavailable, you know. I'll be frank with you, Nan. I've been closed off for years, just like my boxes, just like your father said. Greta didn't know why I was the way I was unless Rocky told her, but I do think she sensed the fact that I wasn't interested in a relationship, so she felt safe with me because the man she's really interested in has the romantic streak of scrub brush. In other words, it was safe to love me because she knew I wasn't going to love her back.''

Nan sidestepped the part about Greta and Rocky and went right to the heart of the matter. ''You're not like your boxes anymore, Davis. What happened?''

He pulled her into the crook of his arm. ''You came back into my life. After I got over the shock of your throwing yourself into my arms the other day and kissing me, it felt as though a bright light had suddenly illuminated the black cave I'd carved for myself.'' She felt him kiss the top of her head and wrap her hand tightly in his. ''Just promise you won't leave me again,'' he whispered.

Nan looked up into his face. ''I promise,'' she said and hoped with all her heart she could figure out a way to keep it.

Davis helped Nan carry her purchases into the diner, then left with the helpful truck driver to take his truck to the garage. As it was six o'clock, Nan turned on the grill, then called her father as she began unwrapping the newspaper-wrapped meat.

''Hi, Dad.''

''About time you called. Where in tarnation have you been?''

''With Davis, as if you didn't know.''

''I have no idea what you're talking about.''

''Right. Well, I'll tell you all about it when I get

home this afternoon. Meanwhile, tell me what your doctor had to say about your leg.''

''It's still broke.''

''Dad, come on.''

''There's nothing to say, Nan. The leg is mending. By the end of the summer I ought to be free of this blasted cast.''

''So everything is okay?''

''Everything is fine. Boris slept on the couch last night. Probably broke a spring. He's going to make me breakfast too, which scares the daylights out of me. I don't think he can cook.''

''He'll manage because you'll tell him what to do. Dad, did you tell the doctor you aren't very hungry? Did he say anything about the weight you've lost?''

''Now, Nan, you don't go bothering a bone doctor with stuff like that. I keep telling you I'm just off my feed for a while. Besides, I don't get enough exercise to work up an appetite. I promise I'll eat a big breakfast. Hey, I heard you made spinach crepes yesterday. Kind of fancy cooking for the Cactus Cup, but everyone seems to have liked them.''

''Everyone?''

''I got a few calls last night. All the regulars think it's great you're home. What's the special today?''

''It depends on what thawed out on me. No, Dad, it's too long a story to go into right now. Wait a second—that reminds me. Boris said Mrs. Calhoun isn't at the house. What happened?''

"Nan honey, Boris just announced he's frying eggs. I've got to go help him. See you later."

Nan smiled as she hung up the receiver. What had her dad done to Mrs. Calhoun?

The ground beef had partially defrosted, so it was spaghetti with marinara sauce, right on schedule. The chickens were as hard as rocks, as were the steaks; in fact, nothing had spoiled. Nan heard a rap on the back door as she closed the freezer door and turned to find Anna Potter standing there with a doughnut, Danish, and pie order. The day had begun.

It proceeded at a pace hectic enough to give Nan precious little time for worrying about affairs of the heart or realizing how tired she was after spending the night in the cramped cab of Davis's truck. Every time the bell over the door announced a customer, Nan looked up, expecting to see Davis, but apparently the trouble with the truck kept him at the garage. She wondered if he'd talk to Rocky while he was there, and if he did, if he could figure out some way to get her silly brother to approach Greta.

Nan was slicing mushrooms to add to the sauce when the bell sounded. Wiping her hands on her apron, she looked up to find not Davis, but his father, Kyle.

"Mr. Todd!" she said. She put both hands on the counter, glad for the support. Kyle nodded stiffly, his resident sneer suggesting he found the diner unsavory, or perhaps it was just the woman behind the counter that forced his nose to wrinkle and his brows to draw together over those cold blue eyes.

He looked around to see if anyone else was in the diner. When he found it was empty, he came to stand across from Nan.

"What were you doing out all night with my son?" he demanded.

"Well, his truck broke down—"

"I thought I told you to stay away from him."

"Please, don't use that tone of voice with me. Davis isn't a small child you can manipulate—"

"Don't you tell me what I can or can't do with my son," Kyle hissed, his pale face suddenly flushed with anger. "That boy has big plans. There's no room in his life for the likes of you. Besides, you're supposed to be caring for your father. In fact, you're supposed to be leaving Sage any day now, aren't you?"

Nan forced her hands to remain still as she fought to control the waver she could feel building in her voice. "I'll leave when my father's condition allows me to leave. As for Davis, I hardly see where knowing me is going to get in the way of his career. I know how he's an artist with wood—"

"Wood! You call that tinkering art? You call building little boxes a career? The boy is going to be a doctor, mark my words. This carpentry thing is a phase he'll grow out of if you just keep your hooks out of him."

"Mr. Todd, I have nothing to say about Davis's future. I never have. What he does is his decision, not yours or mine."

He narrowed his eyes and shook a long finger in her face. "You were after him that summer."

"I thought I only used him to steal drugs," she said calmly. "You'd better try to keep your story straight."

"You didn't get him then, and you won't get him now," he added.

"Davis is almost thirty years old. What right do you have—"

"Every right. I'm his father. Davis will grow tired of being nothing more than a glorified carpenter and go back to medical school. And when he does get married someday, it won't be to a thief and a drug dealer like you. You've got two days to get out of Sage," he added, his voice low and venomous. "If you're still here after the weekend, I'll call the sheriff and my attorney, and I'll tell Davis every detail of what happened. How do you think he'll feel about you once he knows what you did, what the real reason is behind your running away? I told you before—I don't care what happens to me; I won't have Davis's future ruined by anyone."

After delivering these lines, he turned and stalked toward the door. His hand was on the knob when Nan spoke.

"I did not sell Vince Frisk those amphetamines. I

will not live in fear of you any longer, which means I'll have to figure out who did steal them, and I'm warning you, I will. Davis is a big boy now, Mr. Todd, and I think if he knew what you've been threatening me with for five years, he'd have a story to tell of his own, don't you? Unless you back off entirely, I am going to find out what happened five years ago, and I'm warning you that you might not like the truth.''

It was a bluff. Nan knew she could never hurt Davis, never in a million years. She just hoped that Kyle believed everyone else operated with his code of ethics.

He turned to face her, his eyes two cold stones frozen in ice. ''You'll regret this,'' he said. He stared at her for several seconds, and then he added, ''Go ahead, see what I care. You have until Monday morning; then I tell Davis and anyone else in town who and what you really are.''

As the door shut behind Kyle, Nan almost collapsed. She made her knees lock and stood for a moment, breathing deeply. She was desperately tired of letting Kyle Todd affect her the way he did, for even though she'd declared war, she'd done it with shaking knees and a trembling voice. The big question was, what would he do next?

When the door opened again, Nan jumped. She looked up to discover it wasn't Kyle back to exchange more threats; it was Paul Avery.

"I'm glad it's you," she said with a sigh.

"Hello, Nan. Was that old man Todd I saw leaving?" he asked as he settled on a stool. He was wearing a navy suit which set off his deep-auburn hair, a look too polished for the shabby little diner.

Nan managed to nod. Her mouth was impossibly dry.

"Here to rehash old times, I bet," Paul said. "I was talking with him this morning about you and Davis rolling into town right after dawn—"

"How did you know?"

He smiled indulgently. "I get up early every morning and take a brisk walk," he said. "You'd be surprised at the things you notice early in the morning."

"I bet I would be."

"Well, anyway, we were speculating about what you two had been up to."

"You and Kyle?"

"That's right. How about a cup of coffee?" he asked.

Nan's first steps were stiff. She poured Paul his coffee and watched as he took a sip. "Your coffee is sure better than Harry's."

"Thanks. When you told Kyle that you saw me and Davis coming into town early this morning, did you mention the fact that we were being towed?"

"I don't remember," he said over the brim of his cup.

"You don't remember? Didn't it occur to you that

the truck being towed was an important detail and kind of gave the whole thing a different angle?''

Paul laughed. ''Was Kyle angry that you'd corrupted his little boy? That's ripe.''

''That's not the point. What I'd like to know is why you brought it up with him in the first place.''

She didn't get a chance to hear Paul's answer as the door announced more customers. Nan handed them menus and remembered to dump the sliced mushrooms into the simmering sauce. When she turned back to Paul, she found he'd left fifty cents under his empty coffee cup. ''Thanks for nothing,'' she said bitterly as she cleaned up after him. She was beginning to understand why her father and Davis weren't particularly fond of Paul Avery.

By the time Nan scraped the grill with the grill brick, rubbed it down with a burlap sack, and emptied the dirty grease, she felt like death on two feet. It wasn't until she gathered her purse and the leftovers she was planning to heat for Clive's dinner that she realized she had no way home and she'd have to walk. Normally the two-mile jaunt didn't faze her much, but that afternoon it loomed ahead of her like a two-hundred-mile trek through the Sahara would.

She was peering through the front window when she saw Rocky at the corner in his red Mustang, and she hurriedly locked the door and raced outside. She needn't have hurried, as Rocky was apparently headed for the diner.

"Davis sent me to get you," he said through the open window. "Hop in."

Nan was only too happy to comply. "Davis sent you?" she asked as her brother pulled away from the curb.

"He thought you might be kind of bushed. We worked on his truck all afternoon. Between you and me and that lamppost over there, it would have gone a whole lot quicker if he'd have left me alone, but he insisted on helping, said he didn't want to get stuck somewhere again and be as helpless as he was last night."

He cast Nan a swift blue-eyed glance and added, "It didn't seem to me he had that bad a time being stuck out there with you. He was whistling all day long. I haven't heard him whistle in years."

Nan smiled to herself. Kyle's red-faced threats and Paul's sneaking ways receded. She patted her brother's knee and said, "So, did you make a machinist out of him?"

"Ah, Nan, he's hopeless. I mean the guy is smart. and all, and I know he does wonders with wood. What with all those saws he uses, you'd think a car engine would be second nature to him, but it isn't."

"Not everyone thinks cars are people like you do, Rocky."

"Cars and cows," he said, shaking his head.

"There's a combination for you. Say, did you get a chance to talk to Davis?"

"We talked a lot," she said evasively.

"You know what I mean."

"Well, Rocky, you did say he was whistling, so I guess it's safe to assume that the two of us are beginning to look at each other again, and it's also safe to assume we're liking what we see. Is that a problem?"

"Just for Greta," Rocky said, his face turned toward Nan, but while his mouth formed a frown, his eyes glittered with speculation. "I guess she'll get over him," he added doubtfully as he rubbed his sandpaper chin.

"Davis doesn't feel Greta really cares for him," Nan said. "He thinks she cares for someone else."

That earned her a longer look. "Who?"

"You'll have to ask him. Or maybe the best thing to do would be to ask her."

"I can't do that," he gasped.

"Why not?"

He didn't answer, just chewed on the inside of his cheek. They were back at Clive's place by now, and before Nan got out of the car, Rocky cleared his throat. "I haven't been very watchful over Dad," he said.

Nan, of course, had noticed this. "Is that so?"

"While we all were growing up, there was always you and Steve to be the responsible ones. I was the one who went his own way and did his own thing, the one nobody expected to ever amount to much.''

''Rocky—''

''No, let me continue. I don't know why you ran away from Sage before, but I've been watching you since you got back, and it seems to me that there must have been some powerful reason, because it's obvious that you didn't leave because you wanted to get away from Davis. Well, if you can come back here and face whatever it was you left, the least I can do is get my act together and start acting like a thirty-one-year-old man instead of a spoiled kid. I'll paint Dad's house, and I was thinking I could even finish the kitchen so you don't have to do it before you leave. When are you leaving, anyway?''

''I don't know for sure,'' she said truthfully. ''But not right away. Rocky, let me ask you a question. If you heard some really awful rumors about me, rumors spread by a nasty but established member of this community, would you believe them?''

''Rumors that you'd done something wrong, you mean?''

''Yeah, something like that.''

He considered this a moment; then he shook his fair head. ''Nope. Not you. You're my baby sister!''

Nan grinned at him. For the first time in her life she felt a connection to Rocky, and her determination to stop living in fear of the past solidified. ''Thanks,'' she said.

''No problem. Tell Dad I'll be over on Sunday.''

''What did you do to Mrs. Calhoun?'' Nan asked her father.

He was busy opening the leftover containers of cooked pasta and marinara sauce, tasting the latter with his finger. ''Not enough garlic,'' he proclaimed.

''I used all you had at the diner.''

''Harry ran down my supplies, right?''

''I should have thought to buy more.'' The thought crossed her mind that her father was laying the groundwork for the fact that he wouldn't eat much dinner. It occurred to her that the sauce was fine, that it had enough garlic, that he just didn't want to eat. Why?

''That man would have run the Cactus Cup right into the ground if I hadn't fired him and you hadn't offered to take over.''

''You are avoiding my question, Dad. What did you and Boris do to Mrs. Calhoun?''

''Boris wasn't even here.''

''Dad?''

''Well, now, I didn't do anything, not really.''

''You didn't hurt her, did you?''

''Of course not. What a question!''

''Then what?''

''Nothing. She just up and quit.''

"After a couple of hours?"

"Fickle woman!"

Nan sat down and put her hand over her father's. "She didn't strike me as fickle. In fact, I'd wager a bundle there isn't one fickle bone in May Calhoun's entire body."

Clive nodded thoughtfully. "Well, I'll tell you. I got up, and she was here. She talked and talked and talked but, being a gentleman, I didn't tell her to clam up like I wanted to. Then she made the most gosh-awful pancakes you'd ever want to eat. I don't think JoJo's dogs would have eaten those things. Thick as your arm, gooey, spongy—"

"I get the picture," Nan interrupted.

"I couldn't eat 'em, of course, and she got mad. Said if I didn't straighten up, she wasn't going to make me her famous chicken and dumplings. I said I imagined her dumplings would sink to the bottom of the Pacific Ocean and kill whatever they landed on at the bottom, and she got all mad again.

"Later she started vacuuming right where I was going to sit down and read. I can't read with a vacuum roaring in my ears, so I very nicely asked her to vacuum somewhere else, and she got all snippy about it. I asked her who was paying who, and she said no one was paying no one 'cause she was quitting. Now I ask you, is that fickle or is that fickle?"

"How are you going to get around here tomorrow

while I'm keeping your diner afloat?'' Nan asked. ''You can't handle the house alone.''

''Fiddle. You'll be home by dinnertime. Just bring home a helping of the special for my dinner like you did today. For breakfast I'll eat cold cereal, and for lunch I'll eat what's in the fridge. Just don't hire me another baby-sitter, Nan. As long as you're here, I just don't need one.''

Nan stared at her father, alarmed by the desperate note she sensed in his voice. Once she looked really closely at him, it wasn't the only thing that alarmed her. He looked pale, tired, old. She noticed a round bulge in his shirt pocket—it was the exact shape of a prescription bottle. Was he on new medication for his leg? Would that account for his general air of fatigue? All she knew for certain was that this was her father's home, and if he didn't want outside help, then she wouldn't hire outside help. And he was right; the situation had changed. She wasn't leaving.

''Maybe Boris can come over and keep you company.''

''That's a good idea,'' Clive said. ''And you're here, Nan. Now tell me about what happened to you last night. With Davis, I mean.''

''Are you sure you wouldn't rather rest first?''

''No, no, I want to hear everything that happened. I like that boy. I guess that's no secret to you.''

''It's no secret,'' she said fondly, love for her dad filling her heart. ''It all began when your doctor changed the time of your appointment, and Boris coerced Davis into offering to take me into Reno for supplies.'' She told him the whole story, editing here and there when a moment became too private to share. By the time she was done, he was smiling.

Davis called later that night after Clive had gone off to bed to read a spy thriller he'd read a dozen times. Nan took the cordless phone with her into the laundry room, where she could sort clothes and talk to Davis at the same time. She was bone weary before the call, strangely alert the moment his voice reached her ear.

''I missed you today,'' he said.

''I missed you too. I kind of thought I might see you this evening.''

''I had a date with Greta,'' he said. ''Jealous?''

''Did you kiss her the way you kissed me? For that matter, did you kiss her at all?''

''What do you think?''

''I don't think you did.''

''Smart woman. I suppose you're not jealous.''

''Not anymore,'' Nan said as she loaded light colors into the washing machine. ''So, what did the two of you do?''

''We talked, which is all we ever do, and just as I suspected, she managed to turn the conversation to Rocky. I talked about you all evening, so you can just imagine what a party we had.''

"Did Greta admit she's in love with Rocky?"

"I'm beginning to think she's as backward as he is. Has your fertile little mind come up with a plot to unite the two of them?"

"Yep. Rocky is coming over to paint the kitchen Sunday. You bring Greta. We'll go from there."

"As a plan it seems to lack a certain panache."

"Do you have any better ideas?" she asked.

"No."

"I told Rocky that you believe Greta cares for someone other than you. He's absolutely terrified at the thought of there being a third man in the picture. I honestly don't think it crossed his mind that it might be him."

Davis laughed. As Nan joined him, she heard a *clink* against the side of the washer drum. She reached in and extracted the last item she'd thrown in, her father's shirt. The pocket bulged with the cylindrical shape Nan had noticed before dinner. Just as she had suspected, it was a plastic prescription bottle. Nan set it on the dryer and reloaded the shirt. Then she picked up the bottle and held it at an angle to the light.

"Do you know what this is?" she asked Davis after she spelled out the long word.

"It's a painkiller. Why?"

"Dad's taking it."

"Well, a broken leg can be a painful thing. He's lucky he didn't end up in a hospital."

"I thought of that."

She slipped the container into her robe pocket as Davis added, "What strength? How many are in the prescription?"

Nan dug out the container. "Twenty-four, but it says it can be refilled four times. Dr. Bellamy has him taking two tablets three times a day for pain."

"Whoa! That's potent stuff."

"If he's taking all of that, could it make him lose his appetite?"

"I think so. I'd have to look it up to be sure. I hope he doesn't get addicted to the things."

The word *addicted* brought something else to Nan's mind. She paused to collect her thoughts, then began.

"Davis, we need to talk about something very important."

"Okay."

"No, not tonight, not over the phone. I have to work at the diner tomorrow, but tomorrow night could you come over here?"

"My heart is freezing at the tone of your voice. Tell me you're not saying good-bye."

"I'm not saying good-bye," she said firmly. "But we do have to talk about the past and the present and, really, even the future. I want to lay everything on the table. I may be able to offer you answers to questions I've avoided."

"This sounds serious," he said.

"It is. But we have to do it."

"I'll pick you up at the diner after work."

"Okay."

"And, Nancy, I just want you to remember something. I love you. I always have. I suspect I always will."

"I love you too," Nan said and recradled the receiver with infinite care.

It seemed as though the day lasted weeks. Nan did all the chores on remote control. She cooked and cleaned and cooked and cleaned again. Every time the bell over the door rang, her heart skipped up her throat, but Kyle Todd stayed away.

Just when she thought the day would never end, it did, and then all of a sudden she realized that this meant Davis would come, and she began to dread the coming evening and what she had to say. Perversely the minutes that had dragged their feet all day now raced, and then he was at the door and she was locking up.

They rode in silence. While Nan knew why she avoided looking at and talking to Davis, she didn't know why he did the same with her unless he was sensitive to her mood and was giving her the space she needed to marshal the courage for what lay ahead.

Nan heated the special—scalloped potatoes with ham—for their dinner. Clive ate a few bites and quit. For once he didn't make any excuses, and for once Nan didn't make a point of asking him if he was okay. Right after dinner he told her and Davis that he was tired and was going to bed. Davis helped Nan wash the dishes; then they walked outside. Nan took an electric lantern that she found in the broom cupboard and asked Davis if they could go down by the river.

The evening was cool, and the breeze was strong. There was the feel of impending rain, a welcome thing in Sage any time of the year. Nan breathed in the rich air as they threaded their way down the road to the river and over the rocks to the water's edge. Nan remembered a spot under the cottonwood trees that was semi-grassy, and she headed for it, Davis on her heels, both of them still quiet. Only the wind rustling the leaves and the river to their left filled the night air with sound.

Nan found her spot. She sat down, the lantern beside her illuminating a small circle that included a part of the river. The water looked silvery in the strange light as it rushed past; there weren't many rocks at this spot, so it wasn't loud. Davis sat down across from her, his knees almost touching hers.

"This is strange," he said after a few minutes.

"I know."

"I have a feeling we both have something to say that we wished we didn't."

"I knew something was troubling you tonight," Nan said. "I thought maybe it was the melodramatic way I announced that we had to have this talk."

"I have something to say—you're right. But you go first."

"Just promise me that you'll listen to the whole thing."

He promised. Nan took the deepest breath possible, but it didn't help calm her nerves. "I didn't run away from you because I feared your love or the idea of marriage or anything else about you," she began. "I left because your father made me leave."

Davis narrowed his eyes. "You'd better explain that."

She told him about the "incident." She told him how Vince Frisk had accused her of selling him amphetamines, how Kyle had said he had further proof of her guilt, how he'd given her one chance to stay out of jail and she'd taken it. She told him she hadn't realized then what she was giving up, how dreadful it would be, and by the time she did, it was too late and she was too afraid.

As Nan talked, Davis's gaze drifted toward the river. When she stopped, he looked back at her. She couldn't tell what he was thinking, if he believed her, if he'd even absorbed what she'd said.

Finally he swallowed. "What proof did my father say he had?"

"Papers, purchase orders, stuff like that. Davis, someone sold Vince those drugs. I know it wasn't me." She touched his arm and added, "You were the only other person—"

"Are you saying you think *I* sold amphetamines to Vince?"

"I don't know what I'm saying," she admitted miserably. "The idea never even occurred to me until recently. It was something your father said about you and Vince being friends, about Vince owing you a favor for the tutoring you did, and then you said you did some stupid things to try to convince your father that you weren't medical-school material, and it began to add up.

"Davis, in my heart I don't think you were capable of selling Vince drugs, but I have to ignore my heart right now and find the truth, because if I don't leave Sage by Monday, your dad is going to call his attorney and start telling anyone who will listen what he believes I did. That's why we had to talk tonight. I have to find out the truth. I have to figure out a way to clear my name, because I can't leave my father right now. Something isn't right about him—"

"Nancy, I didn't sell Vince amphetamines," Davis interrupted. He took her hands into his; she was surprised to find he was trembling almost as much as she was. "Vince and I weren't friends, not really," he explained. "I did tutor him, but only for half a semester in college. He flunked out, anyway, so you can tell how much he must have appreciated my efforts.

"As for the stupid things I did, they weren't quite that stupid. I got five speeding tickets in a three-month period, for instance. My insurance rates were horrendous until I reached twenty-five. I dated an 'exotic dancer' whose sole virtue in my eyes was that she horrified my father. I cashed in savings bonds and spent the money on some of the tools you saw in my workshop the other day, an act he detested—do you get my drift?

"And then I took a small classload and did poorly and ended up on academic probation, and well, they finally just told me to go home and come back when I was ready to settle down. Stupid things, but things done out of desperation and unhappiness. I didn't sell Vince Frisk drugs out of my father's pharmacy."

Nan heaved a huge sigh of relief. "I knew you didn't. In my heart I knew you couldn't do something like that any more than I could."

"Which leaves one person you haven't mentioned who might have been able to," Davis said.

"Paul Avery?"

"You did think of him."

"Not until yesterday. Would he have had the opportunity? But why would Vince protect Paul by blaming me?"

"Money. If Vince was addicted and Paul sold him amphetamines and then my father discovered it, Paul might have been able to buy Vince off. It would have served two purposes. It would have gotten him off the hook, and it would have gotten you out of town, away from me. Paul was jealous of the way you felt about me that summer. He had Alison, but it was like he wanted you too."

Nan nodded. She thought about all the things Paul had said about Davis and the almost possessive attitude he'd displayed toward her on their one and only date and knew Davis had hit the nail on the proverbial head. For whatever misconstrued reason, Paul was jealous of Davis, and after the sneaky way he'd acted the other morning, it wasn't too hard to imagine him arranging things the way Davis suggested.

Davis had apparently been thinking about the first part of what Nan had told him while she mulled over the last part. Abruptly he said, "Let me get this straight. My father made you leave town without telling me?"

Nan nodded.

"Why would he do something like that?"

Nan had never thought she'd live long enough to see the day she defended Kyle Todd, but the pain in Davis's voice was too hard to bear. "He thought I was guilty," she said.

"An eighteen-year-old girl? Even if you were, what purpose did that kind of heartlessness serve?" As if shot from a cannon, Davis exploded to his feet and walked away from the circle of light. Nan heard him move down the riverbank, and she understood he needed time alone with his thoughts. She'd had years to think about all this; he'd had only minutes, and, to top it off, his father was the one who had caused such anguish.

While she was alone, Nan considered the possibility that Paul had done what she'd been paying for. If so, it meant that he knew why she'd left. It meant that he'd been building his life while she hid from hers. It meant that he'd been conning her since she got back.

Davis reappeared as Nan was about to shout with anger. She sat still as he sank back to the ground.

"We have to confront Paul Avery and my father and Vince Frisk," he said, his voice solemn but determined. "I'll get them each to my house with a different excuse, and we'll get this thing straightened out once and for all. This is going to sound very sad, but I think it will be harder to get my father to come than it will be the other two."

"I know how to get him to come," Nan said. "Tell him you're reconsidering going to medical school. He'd walk on broken glass to get you to do that."

"Still? He said that?"

"Yes." Nan didn't add what Kyle had said about Davis's choice of careers. Maybe when Paul got what was coming to him, Davis and Kyle would find a way of bridging their differences. She suspected she was being overly optimistic.

"He has never understood, but it doesn't excuse the way he treated you."

"Plan it for tomorrow," she said. "Rocky will be with Dad, painting the kitchen, and I can borrow his car."

"I keep forgetting you can't drive a stick shift."

"Once he gets his leg out of that cast, I'm going to get Dad to teach me," Nan said. She saw Davis look down at the grass between them, his mouth a straight line. "What is it?" she asked.

He shook his head.

Nan said, "Plan the confrontation late in the day. We have Rocky and Greta to work on in the morning."

He nodded uneasily. "There's something you don't know, Nancy, something I have to tell you, something that dwarfs what we've been talking about." He held her hands very tightly. "I looked up that pain medication you told me about last night," he continued, the very tone of his voice raising bumps on her spine. "I was right—it is very potent. It's the kind of medication prescribed for very serious pain."

"I didn't know a leg—"

"And then I recalled you mentioning Clive's doctor's name, the one on the label. You said it was Dr. Bellamy."

Nan nodded, unable to speak. She was trembling again. She knew something important was coming, and in many ways, for that instant, she wished she didn't have to hear it.

"Nancy, Dr. Bellamy isn't an orthopedist."

"What kind of doctor is he?" she asked, her voice raspy with fear.

"Dr. Sheila Bellamy is Reno's leading oncologist. That's a cancer doctor, Nancy."

Nan nodded, too numb, too dazed to speak. Somewhere in the back of her mind she'd known all along that something more was wrong with her dad than a broken leg. And here was proof.

Chapter Seven

" "What are you telling me?" Nan asked at last. They'd both risen to their feet and stood staring into each other's eyes.

Davis pulled her into his arms, but she pushed him away. "Are you saying my father has cancer?"

"No," he said. "I'm saying your father is taking medicine prescribed by a cancer doctor for acute pain. Maybe there's an explanation—"

She turned her back to him and stared at the river. For an instant she wondered what was on the bottom of the river, hidden out of sight under the water just as her part of the earth was presently blanketed in darkness. She turned back to Davis and said, "I've got to go back to the house."

He picked up the lantern, and they returned in silence.

Clive was asleep in his bed and looked so frail and so pale that Nan knew she couldn't waken him and ask him the questions that were burning the back of her head. She thought of calling Dr. Bellamy but was paralyzed with fear and uncertainty, just as she had been years before. But years before, she'd had an out, and she'd been able to run away. There was no running away from this.

One thing made sense. No wonder her dad refused to let her go with him to the doctor. Did he go to the oncologist first, then the orthopedist? If he did have cancer, it wasn't necessarily the end of the world, but of course that dream vanished when she considered the strength of the pain medication he was on.

"Boris," she said. "He'll know what's going on."

She had her hand on the phone to call Boris when it rang. She picked it up and heard May Calhoun's voice.

"Miss Hillman? I just wanted to make sure that you don't try to pay me for the half a day I spent with your father."

Nan said, "I hear it was . . . unpleasant. I guess I should have called right away and apologized for the outrageous way Dad acted. He's really quite sorry, as am I."

"Outrageous?" she asked, seemingly startled.

"I'm sorry, Miss Hillman, but I don't understand. . . ."

"All the cracks about your cooking?" Nan prompted.

"Oh, I tried tempting the dear man with my chicken and dumplings, that's true, but he told me not to bother, that he wasn't feeling like eating. He was very polite, every bit the gentleman. He actually paid me for a full week and told me how sorry he was that I'd made the trip for nothing. He told me not to tell you, but I got to thinking that you're the one who hired me, not him, and it wasn't proper. I don't feel right, keeping all this money when I was at your house less than thirty minutes—"

"Thirty minutes?" Nan mumbled, totally confused.

"Maybe only fifteen. Now, I'd like to send back some of the money—actually, most of it—"

"No," Nan interrupted. "Keep whatever Dad gave you. And thanks for your . . . your understanding, Mrs. Calhoun."

"Anytime," Mrs. Calhoun crooned before she cut the line.

"What was all that about?" Davis asked.

"I don't know, but I'm beginning to think I'd better talk to Boris in person, not over the phone."

"I'll take you to his place."

"I shouldn't impose on you . . ." she mumbled.

"Don't be silly," he said, gripping her upper arms.

"Besides, you can't drive your dad's van. Listen, Nancy, I told you that I loved you. Don't you know what that means? It means that what happens to you happens to me, that your problems are my problems and mine are yours. From now on we're in everything together; we're a unit."

Nan nodded as huge tears filled her eyes and slid down her cheeks. Davis wiped them away with gentle fingers. "Let's go," he said, kissing her forehead softly.

Boris lived in a small apartment over Sage's only barbershop. A bank of windows faced the road, and as Davis pulled to a stop across the street, Nan said, "He's not home." It was the first word either one of them had spoken since they left the house.

"Because it's dark? He's probably just asleep."

"No, he always parks that ugly old Cadillac of his right in front. The barber complains that he scares away customers. The Cadillac is gone."

Davis said, "What now?"

"JoJo Wheeler. Next to Boris, Dad is closest to her. I keep seeing the way their heads were tilted together at the house and the conversation we had at her barbecue. She was mad at me for getting ready to leave again, and it wasn't because of you; it was because of Dad. She also got kind of sad when I talked about Dad coming out next summer to spend a while. I think she knows what's wrong with him."

Davis pulled back onto the street, and, again in silence, they made their way to JoJo's ranch. It gave Nan time to ponder the May Calhoun mystery. Why in the world would her father spin such a long, detailed account of something that never happened?

"Looks like we're getting two for the price of one," Davis said as he pulled up behind Boris's Cadillac.

Nan got out of the truck and felt Davis's hand reach out for hers. They walked up the front path, greeted by the little dogs with eager yipping and by the larger dogs with cold noses.

The light came on as they approached. "My early warning system," JoJo said from the door. "Those little dogs announce every visitor. Come on in, you kids. Are you holding hands? Wonderful."

JoJo was wearing a cherry-red jogging suit and gold slippers. She looked relaxed and comfortable. She ushered Davis and Nan into her sunken living room, where Boris was seated on an overstuffed tan couch. Jazz played softly on the stereo, and on the table before the sofa were two half full glasses of brandy. When Boris saw Nan and Davis, he stood. He was wearing white pants and a crisp white shirt, and his dark eyes sparkled in his round face.

"Nan, Davis! How very nice to see you, and together, no less. This is delightful. How about some brandy?"

"I think Nan could use a little," Davis said.

Boris moved through the room with familiar ease, opened a decanter on a side table, and poured dollops of brandy into two glasses. He handed one to Davis and one to Nan; then he sat down on the sofa.

"Have a seat," JoJo insisted as she took one beside Boris.

Nan was momentarily distracted by the sight of the two of them sitting so comfortably together, and she thought she finally understood why her father and JoJo had never married. It appeared that this time Boris had "got the girl."

Davis sat in a chair at right angles to the sofa. Nan remained standing, too wound up to sit. She looked closely at Boris, returned his smile, sipped the brandy, and wondered where to begin.

"Something is wrong," JoJo said suddenly, as though she'd just noticed how distraught Nan was. She sat forward. "Nan? Is it your father?"

Nan nodded. "I have a feeling you mean that question differently, however. He's okay, at least I think he is. He's asleep. I've come to find out why he's taking pain medication prescribed by an oncologist."

Boris and JoJo glanced at each other, then quickly away, which confirmed Nan's suspicion about their complicity in whatever was going on.

"Please. You two are closer to him than anyone else in the world. He's gone to great pains to keep something from me, but if you don't tell me, I'm going to have to go to him. I can't stand not knowing.''

''You're leaving—'' JoJo began.

''No,'' Nan said. ''I'm not leaving right away.''

''If I have my way, she won't leave ever again,'' Davis added.

JoJo's hand fluttered above Boris's sleeve for a moment before lighting. He looked at her, and Nan understood they were trying to decide how much they should tell her.

''Your father had his reasons,'' Boris said at last.

''I'm sure he did. But certainly you can understand my position.'' When they didn't speak, Nan set the brandy snifter on the table and began pacing. ''Ever since I got back here,'' she began, ''there have been subtle hints that something more was wrong with Dad than a broken leg. He hasn't eaten a single meal, he's tired and drawn, he hides his doctors from me, you two talk as though I'll never see him again if I leave— it goes on and on. I know about the medicine now, I know he's seeing a cancer doctor, I know he's getting worse, not better. I assume he has cancer, that he's in pain, that he doesn't want me to know because he's afraid I'll feel I have to stay with him instead of going back to Oregon.''

At this last remark Boris and JoJo exchanged another look, this one accompanied by the first smile of the evening.

''What are you smiling about?'' Nan demanded.

Still, they didn't speak, but after a few moments Davis did.

"I don't know Clive as well as you two do, but I do know him well enough to see that he's gone to a lot of trouble to hide his condition from his family. Even if you believe that's his right, I'd ask you to consider this: Nancy will ask him about this, and he will have to come clean with her. She has rights too. Someday you'll know all the details, but for now it's enough to know she didn't leave Sage because she wanted to, and she hasn't stayed away all these years because she wanted that, either. You two have to decide if it would be better for Clive if you tell her the truth or if she demands it of him."

Nan noticed JoJo's eyes were bright with unshed tears, but the older woman didn't open her mouth.

"Maybe they're right," Nan told Davis. "Maybe this is something I shouldn't ask them about. Let's go, and I'll talk to Dad tomorrow."

Davis was on his feet when Boris said, "Sit down, you two. I'll tell you what you want to know."

"Boris!" JoJo snapped.

"No, dearest, it's best this way. Clive isn't up to many emotional battles, and I suspect Nan's had her share of them lately as well. Maybe if she hears it from me, she'll be calm when he finally gets around to telling her, and he can draw strength from her."

Nan sat on the edge of a chair and said, "You're scaring the daylights out of me."

Boris nodded. "Your dad has cancer; you're right. I know I'm a doctor, but I'm not a specialist, so I'm not going to go into the details, because Dr. Bellamy should be the one to do that, but suffice it to say that your dad's in bad shape and it isn't going to get better."

Nan felt a numbness growing in her limbs, and then she seemed detached from her body, as though she were floating up near the ceiling, watching and listening to strangers whom she felt great pity for. Davis came to stand behind the young woman in the chair with the copper-penny hair. He put his hands on her shoulders, and instantly Nan was back in the chair, facing Boris, Davis's hands a solid reality at the base of her neck.

"Why won't he tell anyone?" she mumbled.

"Nan, this is going to sound crazy, and maybe it is, but it's the truth. I was with him when he got the diagnosis. Most men would have wallowed in self-pity, but Clive's first concern was you. For a long time he'd been worried about you. Steve was off in California, happily married and all, and Rocky was . . . well, Rocky was Rocky, but you were his little girl, and he knew you weren't happy. When he heard he was going to die, the first thought on his mind was that he had to take care of you."

"He's going to die," Nan stated, hating the sound of the words.

"Everyone is going to die," Boris said. "The doctor doesn't know for sure how long your father has, but does she know how long I have or you or Davis? Anyway, your father was determined that what you really needed was to be back here with Davis.

"You see, he'd gotten to know you, Davis, and he liked you, and he was sure you were still in love with Nan. He didn't know why she ran out on you, but the more he got to know you, the more convinced he was that she made a mistake. He asked her to come for a visit, but she refused, just like she did every time he asked. She invited him to Oregon for another visit instead. That wasn't good enough, you see. He had to have her here where the two of you could bump into each other, realize what fools you'd been, and fall back in love.''

"I would have come if he'd told me the truth about his condition,'' Nan said quietly.

"You would have come and been consumed by grief,'' JoJo explained. "Clive figured you'd be too busy worrying about him to pay anyone else any attention at all.''

"This is the crazy part,'' Boris said, continuing the story. "We were driving out in the desert one day last week, out along County Road 36, because Clive said he felt better when he was driving his new car. He swerved to miss a jackrabbit, and the next thing we knew, the car went off the road and hit the only tree for fifty miles. It was an accident.''

"That's how Clive broke his leg,'' Davis said.

Boris looked at JoJo; then he shook his head. "No, son, as a matter of fact, neither one of us got so much as a scratch."

Nan stared at Davis and saw he was as baffled as she was. At last she said, "Wait a second. Dad didn't break his leg? What about the cast—"

"Boris and I made it up," JoJo admitted sheepishly. "I'd put one on my dog last year, so I had all the plaster and stuff, and of course Boris knew the dynamics."

"It would be such an understatement to say that I'm confused," Nan said.

Boris sighed. "When Clive saw how bad the car looked, he hatched a plan. He would tell everyone but the insurance company that he broke his leg. He knew Rocky wouldn't help and that Steve couldn't, and he knew we knew nothing was really wrong with his leg, so he had JoJo whip up a cast, and he called you, and just like he planned, you came home."

Nan stared at the floor a moment, unsure what to make of it all. At last she said, "Then he hired Davis to come to the house as often as possible, and when we didn't get together, he fired poor Harry Mule and sent both of us over to the diner, and on and on and on." She shook her head; she'd been had by a pro, but she felt a smile turning up the corners of her lips.

"So that's the story," Boris finished. "He had to get rid of Mrs. Calhoun because he took the cast off whenever you left the house. He said that was the worst part of the whole scheme, that the cast got too hot and the crutches hurt under his arms.''

''You mean the cast comes off?''

''It has a seam in the back,'' JoJo said. ''If you'd looked real carefully, I'm sure you would have noticed.''

''So he doesn't have a broken leg. All he has is life-threatening cancer, and instead of getting the cancer treated properly, he's trying to arrange my life?'' Nan asked.

''The cancer has been treated,'' Boris said softly. ''There's nothing else they can do.''

Nan nodded woodenly. Somewhere in the back of her mind she'd known that too.

It was strange, but Nan woke up with a lighter heart. It was as though knowing the facts was better than wondering, even though the facts were about as bad as they could get. Still, where there was a spirit as indomitable as her father's, there was hope, and now she could stay and help him.

This thought led to the next. She had to clear her name quietly. She had to get Paul to admit to what he'd done and get Kyle off her back because she wasn't going to have whatever time she had left with her Dad tarnished with innuendo or, worse, legal action.

Clive was sitting at the table, the cast-covered leg propped up on a chair. Nan longed to tell him to take the stupid thing off, but she and Davis had talked long into the night and come to some conclusions. She would let her father tell her what he wanted to tell her when he wanted to. She would wait.

Meanwhile she spent one uninterrupted moment staring at him when he didn't know she was looking. She memorized the lines on his face, the way he held his head, the shape of his ears. She promised herself she wouldn't lose him one moment before she had to, that whatever time remained for them would be happy. Kyle wouldn't take that away—she wouldn't let him.

"You want some toast this morning?" Nan asked, her voice raspy with emotion.

"Maybe a bite or two. Are you getting a cold?"

"Frog in my throat." Nan put the bread in the toaster and jam on the table. She buttered the toast, set it on the table, and sat down opposite Clive. She felt him looking at her.

"You've been crying," he said, his eyebrows knit together with concern.

The man was astute, Nan thought to herself. Indeed, she had spent a good part of the night crying. "Davis and I stayed up too late talking. I'm just tired. Pass the jam, will you?"

He handed her the jam. "So, you two were up late. Seems to me you're spending quite a lot of time with each other."

Nan smiled. She let the depth of her feeling for

Davis flood her eyes so Clive could see it. "I think I'm falling in love with him again, and I think he's falling in love with me. I guess I have you to thank."

"Don't have the slightest idea why you'd be thanking me for that," Clive said, but she didn't miss his little chuckle even though he tried to drown it with a bite of toast. She hid her own smile behind her napkin.

"You know, Nan," he said a moment later, "I turn sixty-eight next month. Sixty-eight. I've been thinking that a man of my advanced years ought to retire. I've been thinking I'd like to get out from under the Cactus Cup."

Nan nodded. She felt in her bones that this was the beginning of the truth, that gradually over the next few days, now that he knew she and Davis were on the right track, that he'd expose more and more until they could all deal with reality.

"I don't blame you," she said casually. "I've only been working there a few days, and I'm tired already." She decided to further ease his mind by adding, "I'm going to call the Board of Education tomorrow. I've been thinking I might like to relocate here. Maybe I can find a job."

His face flowered with pleasure. "Well, there's an idea!" he said and rewarded her by taking a healthy bite of buttered toast.

A couple of hours later Rocky showed up right on time. As he unloaded his painting gear, Nan tried to figure out if she should tell him about their father's condition. It was the one point she and Davis had not agreed on the night before; he thought Rocky was too "flaky" to be trusted with Clive's secret. Nan suspected her brother's flaky days were over. Besides, he was as much Clive's child as she was. In the end she decided she would tell him if Clive didn't come clean within a week or so. Davis arriving with Greta clinched the decision—Rocky was going to have enough to think about today without the burden of his father's illness.

Actually, she and Davis had argued about one other point, and that was the need to carry through with Operation Rocky/Greta on this of all days. After hearing about Clive and before straightening out the mess with Kyle, Davis was reluctant to get involved in another scene. But Nan was determined to get all her problems out in the air and solved. It had become very important to her that the loose ends of the world be neatly tied; she suspected it was because she yearned for happy endings for things where happy endings weren't guaranteed. Still, she hoped this uncharacteristic compulsion she felt to fix everything would clear itself up very quickly.

They waited until Clive had settled between the cottonwood trees on his lounge chair, his book open across his chest as he slept. Rocky was inside on a ladder, stroking white paint onto the ceiling, and Davis, Nan, and Greta were standing around talking to him. Davis was making a big point out of looking everywhere but at Nan, so she figured he wanted as little to do with her plan as possible. There actually was no plan, but she had noticed shock therapy had been very effective on her lately, so on the spur of the moment she decided to just wing it.

"Greta," she said.

Greta looked at her with those clear green eyes. "Yes?"

"Greta, do you like Rocky?"

She smiled. "Of course."

On top of the ladder, Rocky stopped painting and stared down at Nan.

"Good. Rocky, do you like Greta?"

"Of course I like Greta. We've been friends—"

"No, big brother, not as a friend or, at least, not just as a friend. I mean do you love her the way a man loves a woman?"

Rocky swallowed and dropped the paintbrush, which hit Greta's head on its way to the floor. She screamed in shock as paint dripped down her forehead. Instantly Rocky was down the ladder, dabbing white paint out of Greta's hair and off her face with a rag, apologizing profusely.

Greta put her finger against his lips to shut him up. "I'm okay, really. Besides, you didn't answer your sister."

He just stared at her as though his lips were glued shut.

Greta looked at Davis and said, "Does he?"

David nodded. Greta looked at Nan, and she nodded too.

Starting in her eyes and spreading to her mouth, a joyous smile spread across Greta's face. "Well, I'll be," she said very softly.

Before Rocky could respond, Nan felt Davis take her hand. He tugged her outside.

"What your plan lacked in subtlety, it made up for in finesse," he said as he closed the screen door.

Nan peered though the screen before Davis pulled her away. Greta was in Rocky's arms.

"Nan, you little snoop you," Davis said, laughing.

She tore her eyes away from the tender scene unfolding in the kitchen. "I think I deserve one happy ending today, don't you?"

As he looked at her, it seemed to occur to them both that it was almost time to leave, that Kyle and Vince and Paul were due to start arriving very soon at Davis's house. "There'll be more than one happy ending for you today," Davis promised.

"I hope so, but just in case there isn't, let me take one more peek."

He let go of her hand, and she glanced into the kitchen. Rocky and Greta were kissing. She turned to Davis. "Let's go."

Nan walked through the half-finished house, admiring all the high ceilings, the open staircase, the built-in shelves. Davis had just told her the house could be finished within a few months. He'd told her this with his arms around her. Both of them knew their future was linked with her father's future, but they both also knew that Clive wasn't likely to tolerate them putting their lives on hold until he died. Before Davis left, he'd pointed out a room downstairs and called it a guest room, and they'd left it at that.

She sat down on the bottom step of the staircase that led to the second-story loft bedroom. She was doing her last little bit of hiding, waiting for Kyle and Paul and Vince to arrive before she made her grand entrance and scared them all away. Meanwhile there was nothing to do but wait, and waiting gave her time for thinking. With the knowledge that her father's time was limited came a new perspective on the hurtful games someone had been playing with her life. The whole thing was both more important and less important, an inconsistency that gave no comfort.

At last she heard the third car and knew the time for hiding was over. So, for the present, was the time for worrying about her father. She let herself out the back door and crossed to Davis's workshop. She took time to pluck an orange marigold from a tub of flowers and stuff it into her pocket, as though gathering a little drop of sunshine to ward off the nastiness ahead. It seemed a perfectly logical and rational thing to do.

She opened the door, and for a moment none of those assembled noticed her. There was Kyle with his back to her, but she could imagine the pinched bitterness on his face as he realized his son had called him on false pretenses. There was Paul, dressed in a beige suit, carrying a briefcase, loudly complaining about being called out to sell an insurance policy when one obviously wasn't wanted, and there was a stranger Nan assumed was Vince. He silently watched the other two, but he looked so little like the man who had pointed an accusing finger at her five years earlier that she could have met him at a cocktail party and never dreamed who he really was.

Gone was the gaunt, trembling frame. This man was huge—not only tall, but filled out. In fact, he had a little bit of a stomach on him that overhung his brown jeans. The chest of a brown and orange plaid shirt strained at the buttons, and a second chin rubbed against the collar of the buttoned shirt. He didn't look sloppy or seedy, however. He looked prosperous, from the excellent cut of his hair that minimized the effect of his premature balding, to the gold-and-diamond horseshoe-shaped ring that glittered on the pinky finger of his right hand, to the bright shine on his brown leather boots. Obviously Vince Frisk had conquered his addiction and gone on to bigger and better things.

Davis was the first to notice Nan. He smiled a smile of encouragement and held out his hand toward her. She walked to him, her eyes on his eyes, gathering courage as she neared him.

"What's she doing here?" Kyle asked, almost spitting out the word "she."

"She is going to live here," Davis said. "She is going to be my wife."

Davis had never actually asked her to marry him. Nan's insides suddenly felt like the flower she'd just picked, and she put her free hand into her pocket to touch the soft, vibrant petals.

"What's going on here?" Paul demanded. This demand was followed by similar demands from the other two men.

Davis gently pushed Nan onto a stool. "I want you all to listen for a moment," he said. "I'm going to tell you about something that happened five years ago."

"I'm not staying to hear her pack of lies," Kyle snapped as he took a few steps toward the doors.

"Yes you are, Dad." He said it with so much conviction that Kyle actually stopped in his tracks. Nan thought all three of them looked as though they'd rather be somewhere—anywhere—else, but they all stayed.

"This is what happened. Someone sold Vince amphetamines. Dad found out. Someone coerced or paid or bribed Vince into telling Dad that it was Nancy who did it. Dad told Nancy to leave town immediately or he'd prosecute her. Nancy left. Now she's back, and she's not leaving again. It's time for whoever stole the drugs to confess. You're both upstanding members of the community, and I'm sure that would be taken into account.''

Paul's tolerant and somewhat smug smile faded from his lips. He stared hard at Nan and then at Davis, and finally at Kyle. ''Wait a sec,'' he said. ''What do you mean 'both'? Are you insinuating that I sold Vince the drugs?''

''I didn't do it, and Nancy didn't do it,'' Davis answered. ''That leaves you, Paul.''

He laughed, but it was cut short by the set to Davis's mouth. ''Hey,'' he said. ''I didn't sell anyone anything. Kyle had that stuff locked up when I was there. I'm not taking the fall for something you or Nan did.''

''Neither one of us did it, Paul. That leaves you.''

''Like fun it does!''

Nan stopped listening to them. She looked into Paul's eyes and felt a stirring of alarm. He looked frightened and angry, but he didn't look guilty. She looked at Vince. He was staring at Kyle.

Nan looked at Kyle, who was greedily taking in the argument waging between Davis and Paul. Every once in a while he would glance at Vince and lick his lips nervously. She looked back at Vince, who was still staring at Kyle, an expectant look on his face, as though he were waiting for Kyle to say something.

''Davis,'' Nan whispered.

Davis kept on arguing.

She touched his hand. "Davis, stop. Paul didn't sell Vince those drugs."

This caught his attention. "What?"

"See?" Paul shouted. "She did it."

"No," Nan said.

Paul shook his head. "I'm disappointed in you, Nan. You're as crazy as he is, but I'm not going to stand around and be accused of something I didn't do. One word about this to anyone, Davis, and I'll haul you into court for slander." With that he turned on his heels and stomped out of the workshop.

Davis moved as though to chase after him. Nan caught his sleeve. "Let him go."

"Are you sure?"

"Yes."

"But I don't get it. If he didn't sell Vince the amphetamines, then who did?"

"No one," Nan said, her gaze darting between Kyle and Vince.

Vince leaned back against the worktable, his arms folded above his round belly, his lips a speculative curve.

"What are you saying, Nancy?" Davis asked.

"She's saying no one sold me the drugs," Vince said. "Don't you get it? There was no big crime. Nan ran for nothing."

"That's a lie!" Kyle sputtered.

Vince shook his head. "Give it up, old man. I was a kid then, and I needed the money. I don't anymore, and truth of the matter is, I've always felt kind of bad about it.'' He turned to Nan and added, ''Saying I'm sorry doesn't really cut it, does it?''

''No,'' Nan agreed. ''You were a very . . . convincing actor.''

''Being poor motivated me.'' He looked at Davis and added, ''I didn't know there was any connection between you and the girl, or I wouldn't have done it. You helped me out in school.''

''I helped you flunk math,'' Davis said.

''But I'm a professional gambler now. Something you said must have sunk in, huh? Well, so long, Davis. This is a nice place you have here, and congratulations on your coming nuptials.'' With that, he slowly made his way to the door.

Davis looked as stunned as Nan felt. He walked over to his father, his fists tight balls by his side, and said, ''Why?''

Kyle shook his head, but his thin mouth remained closed.

''Because he desperately wanted you to go to medical school,'' Nan guessed. ''He knew you were getting serious about me—it was the town rumor that summer, remember? We were always being asked when we were going to be married. It was just a rumor, but it scared your father so badly, he paid Vince to act like an addict and point a guilty finger at me. I was so young and so stupid, I fell for it. Presto, I'm gone, you're free to leave Sage and go become the doctor your father never could. Isn't that about it, Kyle?''

''Dad?'' Davis prompted when his father remained silent.

''More or less,'' Kyle said at last. He looked up and added, ''It's not too late, son. I can still get you into—''

Davis turned and almost ran out of the building. Nan longed to follow him, but just like the night before, she knew he needed time to come to terms with a father so self-centered, so egomaniacal that he would sacrifice an innocent girl and his son's happiness to fulfill his own misguided ambition.

Nan didn't know what to say to Kyle. He'd robbed her of years, precious years, with her father. He'd wounded his only child, the only man she'd ever loved, and he'd caused her more pain than she could even bear to recount, and still she couldn't think of anything to say to him. Nothing seemed bad enough. Nothing was good enough.

''I only did it for him,'' Kyle said suddenly.

Nan looked into his eyes. For once the cold-blue marble looked shaken. ''You only did it for yourself,'' she said, amazed at how unemotional her voice sounded.

He shook his head, protesting.

''Look around you,'' she added. ''Look at the life he's made for himself. Look at his tools and the beautiful boxes he's built. He even created this house and this workshop, and he did it with his hands, the hands you wanted to guide into a career he didn't want, a career you never had the guts to pursue for yourself. It was *your* dream you schemed and plotted to fulfill, not his. You should be proud of what he's become, not ashamed.''

"It's too late," he said after a long pause, his normally straight spine curved downward as though he'd aged ten years in ten minutes. "Davis hates me," he added miserably. "I don't blame him."

Nan had always suspected she was too soft. There was little in Kyle Todd that she could respect, but seeing him broken gave her no pleasure, either. If it meant he regretted what he'd done, however, it meant that maybe it wasn't too late.

Picking her words carefully, she said, "I don't believe Davis hates you. I think he's horribly disappointed in you for my sake as well as his own. But I think there's a way back too, and I think you can find it if you search your heart. If there's anything I can do—"

His gaze darted to her face. "You'd help me after what I've done?"

She nodded slowly. She didn't add that she'd help because of Davis, not because of him. That was a little too much like kicking a man when he was down.

"I don't deserve your help," he croaked, and then his eyes met hers again, and he whispered something else. It sounded to Nan as if he'd said, "Thank you."

Chapter Eight

"How you can still want a man with the genetic pool I must have inherited from my father is beyond me," Davis said. "In fact, my genetic pool must be more like a toxic-waste dump."

Nan had found him out in the field beyond the workshop, out with the sagebrush. She put her arms around his neck and kissed his throat. "I'm assuming you're a carbon copy of your mother, who must have been a saint to live with your father."

He looked down at her, and Nan felt his arms encircle her waist. "I love you, Nan Hillman. I'm not promising you a real easy future, not at first, not with what we're going to be facing, but at least we'll be together."

"A unit," Nan whispered against his chest. She

dropped her arms and asked him to open his right hand. Into it, she put the crushed marigold and added, "There's always sunshine somewhere, my love."

"There's sunshine in your eyes and caught in your hair," he told her. He kissed her gently, a kiss that hinted at what was to come, and when it was over, he smiled and chuckled rather halfheartedly.

"Is something funny? If it is, share it, please."

"I was thinking that Paul Avery won't be bothering you again, now that he knows you're as crazy as I am."

"There's a definite plus."

"When I think of my old man plotting that little charade in the pharmacy to run you out of town so he could ship me off to med school, I want to strangle him," Davis blurted out.

"Does it help to think he did it out of misguided love?" Nan asked.

"Not a whole lot."

"He did, though. I think he honestly believed his actions were the result of love. And if he tries to rebuild what he's so effectively destroyed, you'll both be the better for it."

"I don't think I can bear to hear you defending that man."

"It does seem strange. But he's going to be my father-in-law, or was that marriage proposal just for shock value, like your former relationship with the exotic dancer?"

Davis kissed her on the nose. "It was for real. You never did answer. Are you going to marry me, Nancy? Are you going to live with me and raise a family and every year, around the holidays, try to convince me that my father isn't the jerk he is?"

"What do you think?" she asked with a slow smile.

"I think you are."

"Smart man."

As the sun settled behind the rolling hills, Davis gathered Nan into his arms. "Let's go to your house. I want to ask your father for permission to marry his only daughter."

"I think I know what he'll say," she said.

"I do too, but I can't wait to see his face."

"And then we'll come back out here and watch the night sky?" she asked. "I want to make a wish on a falling star."

"And what will you wish for?" he whispered.

"Desert magic," she answered softly, "to last forever."